The Southern Grace Series

HIGH TIDE

AT

PELICAN POINTE

GLENDA C. MANUS

To Rewill

Blessings

Glenda Manus

First Original Edition

Copyright © Glenda Manus, 2015

All rights reserved

Publisher's Note
This is a work of fiction. Some characters may be loosely based on actual people that the author knows, in which case permission has been obtained to use these characterizations. Any other resemblance to any actual person living or dead, business establishments, events or locales is strictly coincidental.

ISBN-13:
978-1515217619

ISBN-10:
1515217612

South Ridge Press Publications
2015

Greg Banks, cover designer
Jill Williamson, cover photographer

A SPECIAL THANK YOU

For the women in our Tuesday Morning Bible Study for keeping me grounded.

For my editors, Laura Whittaker and Krista Cook for their eagle eyes and helpful suggestions.

For my friend, Jill Williamson, for providing the perfect cover photo!

For my photographer friend, Cherie Aubrey Steele, for the bio photo. She has a magic camera!

For cover designer, Greg Banks, for always getting it right!

For my friends and family for believing in me.

For my readers for their sweet words of encouragement. Without them, I would have no reason to write.

And especially to God, whose gentle prodding takes me to places I would never dare to go alone.

Proverbs 3:5-6
"Trust in the Lord with all thine heart; and lean not unto thine own understanding. In all thy ways acknowledge him, and he shall direct thy paths."

~The Southern Grace Series~

High Tide at Pelican Pointe

Glenda C. Manus

CHAPTER 1

"*Love one another with brotherly affection. Outdo one another in showing honor.*"

- Romans 12:10 ESV

"Please use it. It's just sitting there empty." Rock looked across his desk at the woman seated on the armchair in his office and found it hard to believe that this was the same person he had tried to avoid like the plague for the past few years. Up until last summer when Miss Edie's name was mentioned, he had cringed and then felt guilty because he just couldn't bring himself to visit this elderly church member. Then the most miraculous thing on earth had happened - well, maybe not on earth, but in his mind, it ranked just shy of the conversion of Paul on the road to Damascus. As he sat and watched her chatter amicably, he reminded himself not to exaggerate, but it was still one of Park Place Presbyterian's most famous miracles - the conversion of Miss Edie.

The 'use it' she was referring to was her beach house, the place where she had been happiest until her husband, John's death. A death she didn't accept gracefully, and had blamed God to anyone who happened to be within listening distance of her scalding hot tongue. And speaking of tongues, it was last year's Pentecost Sunday sermon that had spoken to her, turning her hardened heart into butter.

She had come to his office to offer him the use of her beach house. He realized she had stopped talking and was waiting for his reply. "Miss Edie, that's very generous of you. Are you sure you don't mind us using the house? To tell you the truth, we haven't even started looking at rentals, but our family vacation is only a few weeks away."

"Please," she said. "I want to do this for you and Liz. You've done so much for me."

Her sincerity was heartwarming. He knew if he didn't accept her offer, she would be disappointed. "Thank you," he said. "I can't think of a place we would rather stay. It'll be nice to have some privacy away from the rowdy Clark clan."

She was visibly pleased that he had accepted. "That's wonderful! If you want to be close to your family, there are several large rental houses just around the corner in Pelican Pointe that the rest of your family could reserve - especially since it's so early in the vacation season."

She stood up to leave, but then sat back down. Rock did the same and they both laughed. "Up and down - I feel like we're playing musical chairs," she said.

From her slight frown, Rock could tell there was something bothering her.

"Are you okay?" he asked. "Are you dizzy?"

"No, no, nothing like that," she said. "It's a silly thing, really." She paused for a moment. "But I thought I should tell you anyway. You know last year I let Wanda Burns stay in the house all summer while she was writing her book." Rock nodded. "Have you read her book?"

"I'm ashamed to say I haven't," he said. "Liz has read it and keeps telling me I should, but I just haven't had the luxury to sit down and read for quite a while - maybe while we're on vacation."

She laughed. "I'm not scolding you for not reading Wanda's book," she said. "I was just asking because of what's in the book. Of course, it is fiction and Wanda admits that the actual happenings are wildly exaggerated in the book."

Rock wondered where she was going with this. What did Wanda's book have to do with Edie's beach house? He looked at her expectantly.

"Apparently there were some mysterious things happening on our end of the island last summer. Bonfires, ghost sightings, pets disappearing - that sort of thing. Of course, I don't believe in ghosts but some people do. Wanda nervously laughed it off, chalking it up to pranks by kids on the island with nothing better to do, but when I offered her a week or two down there to work on her new book this summer, she declined – said something about calling ghostbusters."

Rock busted out laughing. "That's our Wanda," he said. "Sometimes she takes things a little too seriously."

His laughter was contagious and Edie joined in. "She does, and sometimes that's not a bad thing," she said, "but I still felt I needed to tell you in case Liz is spooked by things like that."

"Now I understand why Liz was so crazy about Wanda's book," he said. "She loves a good ghost story. In the Lowcountry where she grew up, ghost stories abound. She'll love it."

"Well you never know how people are about those kinds of things. I didn't want anything to ruin her vacation. I had totally dismissed it from my mind until I just now thought of it."

"Then I'll totally dismiss it from mine," he said. "Having a house all to ourselves is going to make Liz happy," he said. "I was afraid she would run for her life when she saw all the people my family tries to cram in two houses. She didn't know what she was getting into when she married into the Clark clan," he said. "And I didn't tell her for fear she'd change her mind about marrying me."

Miss Edie smiled up at him. "Oh, I think she knew. And if she didn't, it wouldn't have made a mite of difference. Her love for you was written all over her face, and still is. You're the only one who didn't notice it."

"I was too busy trying to hide mine," he said with a grin. "I would have never in a million years dreamed I had a chance with her."

He knew their falling in love was a miracle in its own right. As a matter of fact, there were many small miracles that had happened in Park Place in the last year. The members of the town council should make a new sign and replace the old one, saying 'Welcome to Park Place - the small town where miracles happen.' He smiled at the thought.

Edie had no doubt that her favorite minister was telling the truth about not realizing Liz had fallen for him. Vanity was a foreign word to him. She thought back to the times she had made his life miserable and marveled at how quickly he had forgiven her. Enough dwelling on your past transgressions, Edie, she heard a small inner voice say. Don't keep punishing yourself. God's Grace is sufficient. Yes, grace - that was the key.

She looked again at the man who had helped her come out of her hardened shell. Yes, he was handsome and unassuming, and he had no idea that half the women in town had at one time or another had a crush on him. Why, if she'd been a few years younger....

She stood up again. Rock walked around the side of his desk and held his arm out for her. She placed her elbow around his and he walked her to the door. "Paul and I are going down in a couple of weeks to do some deep cleaning. It's one of the older homes on the beach in a place called Pelican's Pointe near the west end of the island. We'll give you a full report on the state of affairs when we get back. Perhaps the ghost has moved on."

He patted her arm. "Ghost or no ghost, we're going to have fun."

CHAPTER TWO

"*B*ut the Lord is faithful, He will strengthen and protect you from the evil one."

- 2 Thessalonians 3:3 NIV

The wind rustled through the tall sea oats as an early morning fog lifted, then settled back down over the sand swept dunes. Two shadowy figures made their way along the beach, stopping every few feet to get their bearings. "It's the Devil's Footpath, I tell you."

They were an unlikely pair. The taller of the two had an unkempt appearance. His long grey hair was thinning and peppered with remnants of red, a dull red, which like the man, was lacking the fire of earlier years. His jeans had holes, not the holes of the fashion-conscious kids about town, but holes of the kind that had been worn too many times and not washed often enough. He had on a decent looking jacket, one he acquired by waiting in line when a local church handed out coats to the needy.

"I came upon the path yesterday. I'd 'bout near forgot about it until my old friend, Martin said you had been asking questions about it. I hadn't walked down here much since that highfalutin' developer that caters to those Yankee snowbirds gated this end of the island off, denying access to the west end nigh on twenty years ago. I'm glad somebody has the gumption to sue 'em." He turned to look at the other man. "Hey, I didn't catch your name."

"Peterson." It was his surname, and a common name on the island. His uncles and cousins had made quite a bit of money in land deals and real estate. Although success and fortune had somehow eluded him, he felt his next big break was right around the corner. He didn't want the old man to know his given name. He had a puffed up view of himself and felt he was above associating with the likes of him. He didn't have many friends and that's the way he liked it. He prided himself on being well dressed. Today, he was wearing a three piece suit with tie, and a pair of black loafers that had been spit shined when he left home but were now sucking in sand as the two of them walked side by side on the beach.

He had inside information that the public access lawsuit wouldn't stand up in court, but for the time being, the gates were down and the winter residents had already gone back north to spend the summer. West End was a seasonal resort named aptly for its location and open September through May. The residents were retirees, primarily Canadian, New Yorkers or New Englanders who leased the cottages to escape the harsh winters up north. This year the resort had closed a month early for some much needed improvements and maintenance.

"I've read stories about the path through old newspaper clippings," he said as he stopped and propped one arm on the sand fence and shook the sand out of his shoes. He watched as his companion walked ahead of him, searching for breaks in the dunes. "Foolish old man," he said under his breath. It was probably long gone by now, this Devil's Footpath, encroached upon by all the fast-spreading underbrush; but if he fueled some flames, it might accomplish his plan - a grand scheme of buying up land for a song that would put him over the top. His family would look up to him for a change.

The old man started waving his long arms in the air. "Here it is, Peterson," he shouted. The wind had picked up and was carrying his voice in the other direction, but from his wild motions, it was evident he had found something. He started forward with the wind blowing at his back carrying him along quickly. Sheets of sand were blowing across the dunes now, seemingly more so with each wave of the old man's arms. By the time he had reached the spot, he'd had to pull the collar of his jacket up around his head to keep the sand from stinging his neck and face.

He bent down to examine the area where the man was pointing. He would have never spotted it on his own. The path didn't appear to have been used in years. Thick, shoulder-high scrub brush made the area around it nearly impenetrable, but as he stooped beneath the brush, a chill descended from his head to his toes as he spotted the large elongated bare spots making a perfect path down from the dunes. It looked as if a prehistoric beast with a long pointed toe had come up out of the sea and stomped his feet as he made his way into the far recesses of the island. It was odd that no grass at all grew within the confines of the 'footprints'. He eased himself back from the path and stood up straight, shaking his shoulders and flexing his arms as if to rid himself of the uneasy feeling that had come upon him. No wonder they called it the Devil's Footpath.

The old man gave him a toothless grin. "Creepy, ain't it?"

This was one point he and the old man could agree on, but he didn't want to admit his uneasiness.

"Where does it lead?" he asked as he buttoned up his coat and straightened his tie.

"Somewhere between here and those houses - Pelican Pointe, they call it, because the land makes a point like the letter V. See how it juts straight out to the water?" The man pointed to a cluster of houses on the thinnest part of the island. They were prime real estate, because they had rows of dunes out front to protect them from beach erosion, and other than the road that divided the island, there were no other houses in the marshy area behind them, all the way to the waterway. The houses all had an unencumbered view of both the ocean and the waterway. "We always played along the path when we were just young'uns. Perry McCauley's old man said there was pirate treasure buried at the end of the path. We dug holes, but always hit water before we hit any old treasure. It ain't but about two feet above sea level. It was creepy back then too, but you know how boys are, daring each other and such, but the path just stops dead right in the middle of the marsh grass - it don't go nowhere."

***

Deep within the confines of the path, about a hundred yards inland, a slim figure knelt in the middle of a clearing. Having a keen sense of hearing, her meditations had been interrupted by voices coming from the entrance to the path. She had been careful to keep the entrance concealed, always slipping in and out, barely rustling the sea oats as she passed. How had they found it?

Jet black hair hung gracefully from her long slender neck, and with her back straight and head erect, one might say she was beautiful. But her beauty, upon closer inspection, was an illusion. It was her eyes, cold and gray - sometimes piercing, sometimes flat that defined her appearance.

She tuned out the sounds, and her lips formed a thin rigid line while uttering an almost inaudible chant. It brought forth something deep and dark, a kind of a presence coming up from her very being.

***

Back at the entrance of the path, the old man stopped talking and stood still, listening. Peterson shook off an uneasy feeling. A path that leads nowhere. A chill came over him again and he started retracing his footsteps toward the ocean. He was glad to get out of this strange place. It was stranger still when he got back out in the open at the edge of the dunes. The wind had stopped blowing and the sun was shining, as if the darkness had never happened.

The old man noticed it too and turned to him. "Seen enough, have you?"

"Yes." He reached inside his jacket and pulled out an envelope. His hand was shaking, but he opened it and plucked out a fifty dollar bill to dangle in the man's face. "Can you keep quiet?"

The old man's grin showed several missing teeth. "Quiet as a church mouse," he said, as he reached out and scooped the money out of Peterson's fingers.

Peterson lingered on the beach for a while after the old man left. He walked past the gazebo that was perched above the dunes on the beach side of Pelican Pointe. All the homes were huge, most were three stories high, except for two older homes whose owners had decided not to jump ship when all the other older homes had been acquired for the development. Even though they were considered to be part of Pelican Pointe, they stood slightly apart from the others.

Those were the two houses he was interested in and by hook or crook, he planned to get them.

CHAPTER 3

"*U*nto *every one of us is given grace according to the measure of the gift of Christ.*"

- Ephesians 4:7 KJV

Edie had been sneezing all morning. The beach house was musty from being closed up over the winter. A layer of dust covered everything and spiders had been busy building cobwebs in all the corners. She had come to Pelican Pointe with the express purpose of cleaning up for the arrival of Rock and Liz, who would be here in less than a month. She had not come alone. Her son, Paul was with her for the week and was helping her clean out John's clothes and the clutter both of them had accumulated over the years. She hadn't had the heart to do it before; in fact, she hadn't set foot in the house since John died three years earlier.

The cottage had been built in the mid '60's. She and John bought it in 1975. A week's vacation on the island had made them want to have a second home here and it worked out well. Edie and Paul, who was about ten when they bought it, would spend summers at the beach house and John would fly down from New York on weekends and any other time he could get away for a few days.

When Paul graduated from college, he went to work in Charlotte, married and had two children. It was to be near Paul's family that prompted John and Edie to move to Park Place, South Carolina when John retired. Their plan was to spend half their time there and the other half at the beach house. All of that ended when John died suddenly of a heart attack.

A knock on the door brought Edie out of her reminiscing. She peeked out the window and saw her neighbor, Charlie Parker standing there with a pie in one hand. She opened the door.

"Well, you're a sight for sore eyes, Edie," he said. "It's been way too long since we've seen you, my friend."

"Come on in for coffee, Charlie, it's good to see you too." He walked into the cozy kitchen and Edie closed the door behind him. This time of the year, the windows were usually wide open with the smell of the fresh sea breeze wafting through the sheer curtains. But the weather had turned off cool and brisk and Edie's bones didn't get along well with the cold damp air.

Charlie used the floor mat to brush the sand off his shoes. "I had to come in from the beach side. The path between our houses has grown up with weeds and underbrush. The sand spurs have grown out of control."

"That reminds me," she said. "I've got to hire someone to clear that all off before my summer guests arrive. I wouldn't want them to get those nasty little buggers in their feet. Is Jimmy Hodges still doing landscaping?"

"Nah, he somehow or another came into some money and bought up some lots and beach houses on the island when the bottom fell out of the housing market two years ago. People couldn't afford their mortgages and the bank did some short selling. When the economy picked back up, Jimmy sold two of the houses, and I heard tell that he made over a million bucks off those two houses alone. He keeps trying to buy mine, but Macie doesn't want to sell. I told her we could have a nice nest egg if we sold, and we could move to Greensboro to be closer to our kids. I'm surprised he hasn't tried to buy yours, with him knowing you rarely come down anymore. His offer's mighty tempting. We're not gettin' any younger, that's a fact."

Edie smiled. She was almost ten years older than Charlie and Macie, and since her soul-renewal last summer, she felt a lightness of heart and step that made her feel like a much younger woman. The walking cane that had been her constant companion was gone - she had no need for it anymore. If she had just realized earlier that bitterness not only affects your mind, but it also plays havoc with your body and soul.

"As a matter of fact, he has written me several letters asking to buy the house and I more than likely would have sold it if it hadn't been for Paul."

"Well, you might be getting more letters. Now, there's a short little weasel type that's been knocking on my door. He claims he's representing Jimmy, but I don't trust him a mite." Charlie looked around. "Speaking of Paul, he came down with you, didn't he? I thought I saw him going out early this morning."

"He did - he's helping me clean out the cobwebs and get rid of some of John's things. It's hard for both of us. He loves this place - says it makes him feel like John's still here, ready to take the boat out for a fishing excursion. Why, he can't even bring himself to take John's white muck boots off the bench on the screen porch. They're still sitting right where he took them off when they cleaned up the boat after their last fishing trip together." She shook her head to brush the memories aside and looked up at Charlie and saw that he was still holding on to the pie.

"Where are my manners?" she asked, and took the pie out of his hands. "This looks delicious - what kind is it?"

"Chocolate Meringue," he said, "my favorite. I asked Macie if we could cut one tiny slice out of it before I brought it over, but she nixed that idea quick like."

"Mmm. Chocolate," she said. "That'll go good with our coffee. Pour us a cup, Charlie. It just finished brewing. I'll cut us a slice of pie."

Charlie took two cups off the shelf and grinned. "That's why I volunteered to bring it over. Macie was going to, but I had a feeling you would see my hang-dog expression and have pity on me." He placed the two steaming cups on the glass top dining table and took a seat in one of the wicker chairs surrounding it. Edie sat across from him and took a sip of coffee. "Hot," she said. "You want some milk to cool it off?" She handed him the cream pitcher and he added a good helping of milk and two teaspoons of sugar.

"The last time Paul was down here, he told us that you've had a rough time of it since John passed away. I wish Macie and I lived closer and could have been there for you."

"Charlie, it was a difficult time, but I'm afraid that I brought a lot of it on myself. I blamed God for taking John away from me just when we were beginning a new chapter in our lives. I wasted some good years alienating everyone around me. I don't know how Paul put up with me, but he was a good son, always there when I needed him."

"Don't blame yourself too much Edie. I don't know what I would do if something happened to Macie - I would go plum crazy, I imagine."

Edie looked at her old friend sitting across from her. She wondered if she would have been just as horrible to Charlie and Macie as she had been to all of her Park Place friends. The two families had been friends for years, having met shortly after Macie and Charlie had bought the house next door.

But yes, she had gone 'plum crazy' as Charlie had said. It wouldn't have mattered who had been in her path. She had felt like God had deserted her in her time of need, but in reality, she had pushed Him away. "Charlie, I don't even want to think back to the way I was. By God's grace, I was able to get my life back. And the two special friends who helped bring about my change of heart are the reason I'm cleaning up the beach house. They're coming here for a vacation in a few weeks."

"Well, we'll make them feel welcome," Charlie said. "Who are they?"

"Reverend Rock Clark and his wife, Liz. They've only been married since last September - really still newlyweds. It was the most exciting thing that's happened in Park Place in quite a while. We had three marriages in one month, and Rev Rock, I guess I should have told you that he's the pastor at our church, was the catalyst in all three."

"Your pastor sounds like someone I'd like to meet. I'll pop over and see them while they're vacationing. I won't bother them, mind you - I'll just introduce myself."

Edie felt a little bad for Rock and Liz. Charlie was not the kind of neighbor who could just pop over, introduce himself and go about his merry way. He loved to talk. Maybe she should warn them.

"I just hope the ghost stories don't scare them off," Charlie said with a grin. "When your neighbor came here last summer to write, she had quite a scare, and Miss Lucy, the name she called the ghost in her book, continued to make a few appearances after she left, but disappeared over the winter. Now I don't believe in ghosts, but this one had us baffled."

"Really? I was under the impression it was probably kids looking for something to get into. Of course, Wanda did seem a little bothered by it all."

"We ordered her book from Amazon," Charlie said. "It reads like fiction and I didn't recognize any of the characters, but the ghost part was just the way it happened, although dramatized a bit for the book. We were surprised when the location in the book was on the coast of Maine, but on her acknowledgement page, she did say that she got her inspiration from our island." Charlie beamed with pleasure. "She even mentioned me as one of her sources of information!"

"I noticed that."

"Macie and I enjoyed getting to know Wanda. It was a nice thing for you to do letting her stay in the cottage all summer."

"It's the only kind thing I did in my bitter years," she said. "You and Macie wouldn't have wanted to be around me after John died. I just about withered up and died myself, I was that angry with God. John and I only got to enjoy the cottage for a year after he retired, and then he was gone. Like I said earlier, I was quite difficult and wouldn't let anyone in the bubble I built around myself."

"That's hard to believe, Edie, but people handle grief in different ways. I'm just glad that you're here now and you seem to have accepted things for what they are." He looked around the room as if seeing it for the first time. "I had forgotten all the changes you made to the cottage. It's bright and airy in here. I remember how dark the paneling was before you remodeled, just like all the beach houses that were built or remodeled during the dark panel days of the late sixties and early seventies."

Edie loved what the decorator had done with the place. Before they moved south, they fixed it up with modern appliances and painted the dark paneling an ocean blue. The cottage was what John called a 'shotgun' house. He joked that it was so open, you could stand at the front door and shoot a gun straight out the back door without hitting anything. The kitchen was on the street side with the dining table separating it from the large open living area that faced the beach. It originally had four small bedrooms, two on each side with a bathroom in between, but they took the walls down between the rooms on the left hand side and made one large master bedroom with a master bath on the end. On the other side of the house, one of the bedrooms was made into a library with a Murphy's bed on one wall and a fold-up cot stored in the closet, to be brought out for the grandchildren when they came for vacation. The other bedroom on the beach side was remodeled and served as Paul and Barbara's room.

"Paint makes a huge difference, doesn't it? John was going to have the house sheetrocked all over, but the decorator suggested that light colored paint would do wonders for the paneling, and she was right. It still gives it a cottage look, but brings the light inside. It saved us a lot of money too."

"Tell me about it," he said. "We did sheetrock, and yours looks every bit as good as ours - maybe better." He stood up. "I didn't mean to stay so long. Macie's gonna start a man hunt for me." He grinned. "Don't make yourself a stranger, Edie. Come visit us."

Edie watched as he walked out the door. They had all been such good friends over the years. She remembered the bridge games and her walks on the beach with Macie picking up shells. Maybe it would do her good to get back in the groove of coming down to the beach house again. She caught herself singing as she picked up the tea cups and saucers and put them in the dishwasher.

CHAPTER 4

"*Behold, children are a heritage from the Lord, the fruit of the womb a reward.*"

- Psalm 127:3 ESV

Edie watched Paul as he carried a laundry basket filled with John's clothes to the car. When she had called Hope House, they said they would be glad to take the items and sell them in their store, a charity shop whose funds were used to support a local battered women's shelter. This was Paul's second trip there, carrying everything from clothing, shoes, old fishing equipment and even a few books from John's library.

Paul looked more like his dad every day, especially now, wearing John's favorite jacket. This cleaning up and out had been hard on both of them. He was in a melancholy mood this morning. She realized now that he had been so busy trying to soften her grief that he hadn't taken the time to fully grieve the loss of his father. Maybe after the work was finished, she could talk him into taking the boat out. She hadn't realized how much she missed boating down the Intracoastal Waterway with its secluded coves teeming with fish and waterfowl, and its tall green marsh grass turning the color of pure spun gold at the end of the day. The Golden Hour, that's what John had called it as the sun lingered over the grass for its final shining moments in the sky.

Paul walked back through the door, wiping the sand off his feet on the rug. "I think I can fit one more box in the car," he said. "How much more do we have?"

"I can't believe you've been able to get everything in, but that's exactly what we have left." She pointed to the box on the floor and a hanging bag that John kept his one good suit in for going to Church.

"I can fit that in," Paul said. "I'll be back in thirty minutes or so. Do you want to go out to lunch somewhere and celebrate getting all this done?" All that's left to do is put a new handle on the toilet, fix the leak under the sink, nail down a few boards on the walkway to the beach and it'll be ready for our guests."

"Let's wait until tomorrow to do the repairs. How about if I fix us a light lunch while you're gone? I was hoping we could take the boat out if that's okay with you. I would love to cruise up the waterway this afternoon, like we used to do. We could dock in Southport and have dinner at the Fishy Fishy Cafe. We haven't eaten there in years."

Paul's eyes lit up. "I'm glad you're finally wanting to get out and do things," he said. "That sounds like just like the break we need. This has been tough."

"Yes, it has." She hugged him. "I don't know what I would have done without you, Paul. I could have never done this alone."

He hugged her back. "And I wouldn't have let you."

As he made his way down the flight of steps, Edie grabbed a tissue and sat down at the table and sobbed. After a few minutes she got up, feeling better for the good cry. Paul was right - it had been a tough few days. She rummaged in the refrigerator and found some deli chicken and some salad fixings. She found herself looking forward to their afternoon adventure. She was going to have to get out and start socializing. She could start with her friend next door.

Before she could change her mind, she picked up the phone and called her old friend, Macie. She answered on the third ring. "I'm ready to go shopping!" she said.

"Praise God!" Macie said. "I thought I had lost my shopping buddy." Before the end of their conversation, they had made plans to go shopping at the outlet stores in North Myrtle Beach the next morning and Charlie would come over and give Paul a hand with the repairs. She smiled and started singing, "I once was lost and now I'm found, was blind but now I see."

***

Edie had forgotten the peace and serenity she felt cruising up and down the Intracoastal Waterway. After leaving the marina where the boat was stored, they made their way north to the Lockwood Folly Inlet and beyond toward Oak Island and Southport. It was a marshy and natural terrain, with little creeks and estuaries all along the space between the barrier islands and the mainland. Docks and fish houses along the way were marked by colorful flags and by the tall masts of the shrimp boats docked there until shrimp season opened again.

She and John had loved to bird watch as they made their way up the Lockwood Folly River. Pulling in and out of the little coves, they would see egrets, pelicans, osprey, Canadian geese and on occasion a Great Blue Heron.

Edie had always favored the waterway over the ocean when boating. The ocean made her uneasy. They had been out once when a sudden squall came up and the waves were coming in over the bow of the boat before they could get back to shore.

The tide was low and some places were just inches deep. Paul knew the waterway well enough not to run aground. Channel markers helped with navigation. Although she knew the markers well, each time they had gone out, John would explain to her that the red channel marker should be on your left going north and on your right returning south. He had told her to always remember *red, right, returning* and she would be safe, as if she would ever go out by herself. She could almost hear him saying it now and it made her smile.

The docks at Southport were relatively quiet as they made their way back to the boat from the restaurant. The tourist season hadn't yet started. In the summer the restaurant would be packed every night with a line waiting outside. There was still plenty of daylight left as they made their way south back to the marina. Paul watched his mother as she scanned the marsh grass and low hanging trees for birds. The look of contentment on her face was a good thing to see. She hadn't looked this happy in a long while - much too long. When his family came down in July, he would insist she come with them. This trip had done her a world of good.

***

"Sorry, I can't get down on my knees and help, Paul. The doctor says I need a new knee, but I haven't got around to needin' it bad enough to cause me go through the pain. I can supervise up here and hand you something if you need it, though." Charlie stood watching with a toolbox in his hand.

Paul was lying on his back, looking up at the pipes under the kitchen sink. "That's okay. I think I'm going to call a plumber. These old pipes look like they're going to fall apart any minute. I've tried but I can't pry this fitting loose and I'm afraid I'll make a bigger mess than it's already in." He wriggled back out and stood up. "At least we got the toilet handle changed in the master bathroom and the new showerhead put on." The two of them had tried to nail down the loose boards on the walkway, but they were so weather-warped, they just popped back up again. "I'm going to get someone out and replace all these old boards. The walkway is a safety hazard and our pastor's wife is pregnant. I wouldn't want anything to happen to her." He got a pitcher of lemonade out of the refrigerator and grabbed two glasses and put them on a tray. "Let's go sit out on the screen porch. I'm glad it's warmed up some."

The porch was still in good shape. John had covered it and screened it in just a few years back. Paul set the tray on the wicker coffee table and poured two glasses and they both sat down. He noticed Charlie looking at the muck boots on the bench near the door.

"I just didn't have the heart to move them," he said. "It was the very last thing Dad did before we left the beach house the last time we were here together. We had washed the boat and were ready to leave when he realized he needed to put them up. He ran up the stairs, put them on the bench, latched the screen door and came back down to his truck. He was ready to get back home to see Mom. The next day was his 73rd birthday."

"You just leave them there. They look perfectly natural on that bench. Why don't you get a little plaque to nail on the bench as a memorial? Keep them oiled where the rubber won't crack and you'll always have that memory of him right in front of you - and for your kids and grandkids too."

Paul looked up and smiled. "You're a man of wisdom, my friend. I think I'll do just that."

Charlie leaned over from his sitting position and looked down the beach with a puzzled expression. Paul turned around and followed his gaze. "What is it?" he asked.

"I don't know." "I was watching a man walking along the edge of the dunes way down near the West End Resort and all of a sudden, he seemed to just disappear." He turned back to Paul. "I don't know, maybe I'm seeing things. I've got this cataract on my left eye and I don't see as well as I used to." He flexed his left shoulder. "Eyes, knee, shoulder - everything on my left side is just giving up on me. Take my word for it Paul. There ain't nothing fun about getting old."

Paul stood up and studied the dunes behind him, thinking it odd that Charlie had seen the exact same scenario that he saw yesterday.

Charlie sat back down and took a big swig of lemonade. "Yesterday it was coffee weather and today it's warm enough for lemonade. It's funny how the temperature here at the beach can change overnight." He swirled the ice around in the glass and looked at Paul. "Do you believe in ghosts?"

"I don't know. Sometimes I feel Dad's presence all around me. It's usually when I'm having a bad day and it's almost as if he's trying to boost me up. But that doesn't mean I believe in ghosts - I don't really understand it but I think it's his spirit." He looked at Charlie curiously. "What brought that up?"

"Have you heard the ghost stories circulating here at the Point?"

"Are you talking about the ghost in Wanda Burns' book? That was just fiction, Charlie. She wrote a novel and she's working on another one now."

"Well she might of written it as fiction, but she got her inspiration from all the strange happenings around here."

Paul laughed. "Maybe one of those nor'easters blew old Blackbeard's ghost down here from Ocracoke. I've heard ghost stories from the Outer Banks and from the South Carolina swamps and marshes, but I didn't know we had our own here at Pelican Pointe. What is it that this supposed ghost does?"

"That's a good question. No one quite knows what it does. It just appears to people as a white flash or a shadow. Mrs. Burns is the only one who's seen anything tangible. She said that on one moonlit night, she saw the silhouette of someone walking through the marsh grass back there." He pointed in the direction of the waterway. "There were also a few sporadic nights of bonfires. I went out there a time or two, but the shrubs and yucca plants are so thick through there, I couldn't find anything. I came back with so many scrapes and scratches, Macie thought I'd found the ghost and fought with it." He grinned. "If I'd been thinking I would'a made up a good story about me tumbling around with a ghost. There's been a few more instances of spotting a fire out in the marsh grass by teenagers walking the beach at night."

"I haven't read Wanda's book yet, but I know Wanda very well - she goes to our church - otherwise I would think that the book fueled the flames of imagination around here."

"Oh no, the stories started before Wanda visited our island. Paul, have you ever heard of something called the Devil's Footpath?"

"Oh yeah, when I was a skinny little kid, a newcomer on the block, the local kids would taunt me and say they were going to going to carry me on their shoulders and dump me on the Devil's Footpath. I stayed inside a lot that summer. Mom couldn't understand why I didn't want to play with the other kids." He put his empty glass on the table. "You want more lemonade?" Charlie shook his head, no, and Paul continued. "The next summer I had shot up a good 6 inches and I wasn't a skinny kid anymore. They didn't threaten me with the footpath story anymore."

Charlie laughed. "I remember that summer. Macie and I didn't even recognize you when you came running over to our house to let us know y'all were here."

"I haven't heard anything about the Devil's Footpath since. I figured it was just something the boys did to scare us skinny little kids."

"I don't know much about it either. I always heard it was a strange path that leads down into the marsh grass. Supposedly the path consists of large bare areas that look like the steps of a giant foot - all pretty much identical. I've got to admit, I've meandered about out there looking for it, but like I said earlier, it's so grown up with those spiky little plants, it would be hard to find if it did exist. And I have trouble believing something if I can't see proof of it."

"I agree. It's probably just a local thing to scare the tourists. Where is this path supposed to start?"

"Well, it's said that it starts at the dunes somewhere between here and the gated community – or beyond the gated community. Like I said, no one really knows." He looked out the window and pointed to the section of the beach to the west. "They're so strict about who comes in and out of there and it would be a long walk down the beach to find it. The gate's down now because of some sort of lawsuit. Maybe it's time to go for another search."

"I might just do that the next time I'm here." Paul stood up and picked up the glasses off the table. "I've got to go call a plumber and a carpenter. Why don't you come back into the house and we'll play a game of cards or something."

"Nah, I've got to get on home. It's almost time for Matt Dillon to come on."

"Ah, Gunsmoke. I remember watching that as a kid. I didn't know it still came on."

"Just on the Western Channel. Macie fusses at me every month when we get the cable bill. I can't help it - it's the only thing decent on TV to watch." He opened the screen door that led down the steps to the outside. "Thanks for the good company and lemonade. I'm sorry I wasn't much help to you."

"You can be a help if you don't mind doing it," Paul said. "We've hired someone to clean up the sandspurs and do a little landscaping out front." He reached in his pocket and pulled out some money. "They can't do it until next week and we can't hang around that long. Just keep a check on their progress and pay them when they finish." He handed the money to Charlie. "If they don't do a good job, let me know."

"Sure thing," he said, and took the money.

Paul watched as he made his way down the steps holding on to the handrail. His mother would have a hard time getting up and down those steps in a few years. Installing an elevator might be the answer - no, that could wait. He wasn't even sure if his mom was going to keep the house. She had mentioned selling it quite a few times since his dad's death. He looked around him. The upkeep on these older houses was expensive, but once he got the plumbing done and the boardwalk taken care of, there shouldn't be anything major for awhile. Maybe he would buy it if she decided to sell.

CHAPTER 5

"*May the God of hope fill you with all joy and peace in believing, so that by the power of the Holy Spirit you may abound in hope.*"

- Romans 15:13 ESV

Edie stopped every now and then to pick up a pretty shell or a shark's tooth as she walked on the beach one last time before they headed back home to Park Place. By the time she got back to the house, she would have walked a full mile and she had only met one man on the beach. She and John had driven it once and it was exactly one half mile from the windsock at the end of their boardwalk to the American flag flying in front of the clubhouse in the West End gated resort.

She had set out walking alone while Paul was busy with the carpenter finishing up the hand railings that led down to the beach. She hadn't realized what poor shape the boardwalk was in until Paul pointed it out to her. She stooped to pick up a pretty conch shell. This one was as smooth as glass, there was no way of knowing how long it had been on the ocean floor being polished to perfection before being spit out upon the shore. It reminded her of how God uses the grit and sands of life, polishing us up before being admitted into His kingdom. Lord knows, she had needed polishing from the inside out. Her pitted and gnarled soul had been transformed because of God's grace and she was grateful.

She had gathered the shells in a small basket. It was the same basket she had used over the years gathering shells when Paul was a child and then later with his two children. It wouldn't be long before Paul's granddaughter, little Mary Grace, would be picking up shells in the same basket. She hoped she would be around to see it. Maybe she still had a few good years left - she felt young at heart even though she had just turned seventy eight. She had been inactive during her grief and her health had suffered for it. Up until last year, she had walked with a cane, but finally getting up and doing for others had given her strength in body and soul. Now she considered herself almost as fit as she had been in her sixties. The cane was gone, hallelujah!

She looked ahead to see how far she was from the half mile mark but apparently the flag had been taken down until the winter residents came back. She could see the empty flagpole up ahead. There were two sailboat dinghys pulled up near the dunes right in front of her. It looked as if they had been abandoned for quite a while. It was time to turn around. She would pick up the pace going back - she'd doodled around long enough. As she turned around, she caught a flash of something white out the corner of her eye. She kept her eye on the spot where it had been and saw it again - this time it appeared to be floating just above the tall marsh grass - then it was gone. She picked up her speed walking back to the house, trying to see where it went but saw no sign of it at all. Odd, but it must be a white plastic grocery bag, picked up by the wind and moved along. She shivered, even though the sun was shining and the temperature was in the seventies. Things just didn't feel right. She'd never had this uneasy feeling in all the years they had been coming to the beach house.

Last night she had seen a light coming from just about the same spot. It was one of those nights that she lay in bed, not being able to sleep, but not wanting to get up for fear of waking up Paul. She had finally got up and gone to the kitchen to put the tea kettle on. With a cup of herbal tea in hand, she walked to the library and sat down at John's desk. During the day, the chair offered a perfect view of the marsh but last night the moon was just a sliver in the sky and the stars were out, bright and clear. As she looked down upon the sea oats and marsh grass, she saw in the distance a light, then realized that it was a campfire burning. It was a small fire, barely visible.

Now that it was daylight, she wondered how anyone could have gotten in there to build a fire. Kids, maybe, but what were they doing in such a place as that? It was so overgrown. There was a public ordinance though, prohibiting having campfires on the beach. She would tell Charlie to have someone check it out after they left.

She was glad to see the windsock up ahead that marked the boardwalk to the beach house. The carpenter was gone, but Paul and Charlie were standing on the bottom step admiring his handiwork. They stood aside so she could walk up the steps. "No more splinters in your hands," Paul said.

Their walkway stood out among the other beach house walkways. The boards were a warm blonde, rather than the drab weathered gray of the others. "It looks nice," she said.

Charlie spoke up. "Now Macie's going to be after me to put a new one up. Y'all are going to cost me a pretty penny, I know it!"

"Yours looks fine," Paul said. "Your boards are not all warped and cracking like ours were." He turned to his mom. "Do you have everything ready for me to pack in the car?"

"Almost – I have everything except my cosmetics bag. Give me ten minutes to wash the sand off my feet and freshen up. Oh, by the way, I saw something a little strange while I was walking along the beach. Something white was gliding along the top of the marsh grass about fifty feet back from the nearest dunes. I thought maybe it was a white grocery bag, but come to think of it, I'll bet it was one of those white egrets flying along the surface of the grass looking for a mouse or something. I hadn't thought about that, yes, I'm sure that must have been it." In her rush to get ready to go, she forgot to tell Paul and Charlie about the fire.

She walked on up the steps with her basket of shells. Charlie and Paul looked at each other. Paul shrugged. "Maybe she's right - it could have been an egret."

Charlie looked skeptical. "The water never comes up that far, even at high tide. It's a good hundred yards to the Intracoastal Waterway. Egrets prefer fish, not mice. And there's never a shortage of minnows and small fish in the waterway."

CHAPTER 6

"*Husbands, love your wives, as Christ loved the church and gave himself up for her,*"

- Ephesians 5:25 ESV

Liz Clark eased her feet over the side of the bed and felt around for her bedroom slippers. The alarm clock on the bedside table had been a thorn in her side since 2 a.m. The red digital numbers taunted her with their agonizingly slow turnover of minutes as she tried her best to get back to sleep. But sleep would not come even though she tried every relaxation technique she had been coached in by all the well-meaning women she knew. Even Madge Price had jumped on the bandwagon, telling her to watch a Youtube video of some breathing technique she remembered seeing on a website called nomoresleeplessnights.com. After she watched the video and breathed along with the narrator, she conked out on the sofa with her laptop, but when she got up to go to bed, she was wide awake again.

She didn't bother turning on the lamp. The streetlamp cast enough light for her to see clearly inside the room. Rock, her husband of less than a year, slept soundly in the bed she was now getting out of. She watched him for a moment as he slept and thought again, as she had done many times before, how blessed she was that God had given her a second chance at love. Ron, her first husband had died of a heart attack when he was only forty-five and she in her mid-thirties. Their best friend, the Reverend Rock Clark, had felt it his duty to watch after her in their mutual grief, and the affection and friendship they felt for one another had taken a romantic twist, leading to a quick turn of events - first marriage and not long after, the joy of finding out that they would be parents.

It had been a fairly easy pregnancy after getting over the initial fear of hearing from her doctor that at the age of thirty-seven, her pregnancy was considered high risk. But now, at the beginning of her third trimester, she was feeling more at ease, especially since the blood work and ultrasounds had shown no abnormalities in the baby's development.

She got up and walked over to the alcove they had set up as a nursery. During the remodeling of the parsonage, the contractor had added a new walk-in closet by extending the room out, then opened up the wall of the former closet to use as a nursery until the baby was ready for a room of its own. She switched on the whale night light plugged into an outlet and stood there admiring the way it was set up. She had done this so many times before, she should have the scene memorized. They had purchased a crib with a built-in changing table. It had drawers and other storage space underneath. That space, plus a matching dresser, held the baby items they had been given when the church gave them a baby shower just the week before. Liz ran her fingers across the side of the crib. She had been tempted to go ahead and dress up the crib with the nautical themed crib set her mother had given her, but it was a little early for that. She picked up the blanket draped over the crib rail and held it to her face. So soft and cuddly!

She made her way into the bathroom and silently closed the door so the sound and light wouldn't disturb Rock's sleep. No use in having both of them wide awake - he would fuss over her and insist on making hot chamomile tea, and frankly, if she had to drink one more cup of hot tea during her pregnancy, she would throw up. She turned on the light and looked at her reflection in the mirror. She examined the dark circles under her eyes and the slight scowl on her face. Yikes, she looked nothing like the person who had considered herself blessed two weeks ago when she and Rock had gotten an excellent report from Dr. Anderson. "You're doing everything right," he had said during his examination. "This baby's as healthy as a horse!" She had laughed and told him she felt a little like a horse herself, with all the weight she had gained. He assured her that an eighteen pound weight gain at this stage was right on target and nothing to worry about.

She splashed water on her face and looked in the mirror again. She smiled which improved the reflected image remarkably. There, that was much better. She practiced smiling again. What a difference it made rather than fretting, worrying and frowning. She had to admit, she'd been hard to live with all week, and why? - just because she had lost a little sleep? She should be enjoying every step of this pregnancy, it may very well be her last one. If she just didn't have to go into work so early every morning. She turned off the light and opened the door. Wait a minute! She closed the door and turned the light back on. That's it! When she looked at her reflection this time, her smile was genuine. She turned off the light, went back to bed, and slept like a baby until the alarm sounded its wake up call.

***

"Wow, you look all cheery this morning," Rock said as he came back into the bedroom from the kitchen carrying two cups of steaming coffee. "Here's yours, cream and sugar." She took it from him, dazzling him with a smile. "You must have slept better?"

"Finally, I did," she said, "after I had an epiphany during the middle of the night."

"Hmm..," he said. "Let me guess." He drew her into his arms. "An ancient, never discovered Chinese secret cure for insomnia came to you in a dream?"

"Close," she said, pulling slightly back so she could see his eyes.

"Well, are you going to tell me or am I going to have to stretch it out with more guesses?"

She put her coffee on the small table between the two reading chairs in the bedroom. "I'm going to tell you, but let's sit down and enjoy our coffee."

"That serious?" he said, sitting down with his cup in his hand. He looked in her eyes trying to gauge her expression.

"I think you'll be pleased," she said, "but I want your opinion. I've pretty much made up my mind, but if you object...." He looked at her expectantly.

"I want to quit my job, and I don't want to wait for the school year to end, Rock. I'd like to put in for a leave of absence today, with as little notice as possible. There's a new guidance counselor in the county looking for a job. Dr. Baker's already talked to her about taking my position while I'm out next year. I think she'd jump at the chance to start now."

Rock was thrilled, but didn't say anything as he watched her look down at her coffee, then back up at him. "I'm sorry, I'm just prattling on. I haven't even given you a chance to say anything. You know, we've talked about me not working when the baby comes, but I haven't given it serious consideration until now, because I've always loved my job. You know that Ron had a generous life insurance policy and also invested wisely over the years. That combined with your salary, we can afford to live comfortably without me working." He still hadn't spoken and she shifted uncomfortably. "Well, what do you think?"

He shifted in his seat, then reached over and took her hand in his. "I think, Mrs. Clark, that you have had an epiphany indeed, much better than an ancient Chinese secret for sleep. Why didn't we think of this earlier?" She shrugged and shook her head. "Now," he said, "if you have problems sleeping at night, you can take naps during the day. Problem is, I might be tempted to leave the office and join you for your naps."

She laughed. "Then I'd never get any sleep." She felt as if a weight had been lifted from her shoulders. She had another thought. "And I'll have plenty of time to prepare for our beach trip with the Clark Clan. It's only three weeks away. I need to get busy!"

Rock was relieved. He had mentioned her quitting work one time before, but she balked at the idea. He was still new at this husband stuff and was glad he'd waited until it was her idea. Cap Price had given him some excellent marital advice a while back. "To keep your marriage brimmin', with love in the lovin' cup, whenever you're wrong admit it, whenever you're right shut up." So far it had served both Cap and himself quite well.

***

Egg and Cheese on wheat - how many times had he fixed this combination breakfast sandwich, the latest of Liz's cravings? Every weekday for the past month, he was sure of it. The month before it had been peanut butter and banana mixed in with a bowl of oatmeal. They had established a routine since they moved back into the remodeled parsonage. He got up when the alarm went off to fix her something nutritious for breakfast while she took her shower and got dressed for work. She had been in the habit of eating a cereal bar on the go in the mornings, but when she'd complained to Dr. Anderson at one of her appointments about a clogged digestive system, he had nixed her cereal bar and advised that a protein, dairy and whole grain diet plan to start the day would help fix the problem. For some strange reason, she had wanted the same exact meal for breakfast every day until she grew tired of it and moved on to something else. He had been convinced he could do the scrambled egg, with grated cheese on wheat toast with his eyes closed, but when he, on a whim, tried it one day, he had burned his hand on the skillet - a tidbit of information he hadn't shared with Liz.

Liz walked into the kitchen just as he had poured them both a glass of milk and pulled his Pop-tart from the toaster. "I can't believe you'd choose Poptarts over eggs and cheese," she said as she pulled a barstool out and sat at the counter where he had placed their plates. He pulled the other stool out and before sitting down beside her, he turned her face toward his and gave her a quick kiss.

"And I can't believe you eat the same thing, day after day," he teased.

"You know, I am getting a little tired of it," she said. "All of a sudden, I've been craving livermush. I'll stop by the Piggly-Wiggly on my way home this afternoon and get some. You'll have something new to cook tomorrow."

Livermush - he was sure he would gag. That's what he got for opening his big fat mouth.

His days of getting up early and cooking breakfast were soon coming to an end. The county had approved her leave of absence, hired a new counselor and she had three more days to work. Hallelujah!

CHAPTER 7

"**K**now well the condition of your flocks, and give attention to your herds,"

- Proverbs 27:23 ESV

"Have you found anyone to preach for you while you're on vacation?"

At times he got aggravated that Reva reminded him of things over and over, but he was grateful at the same time. Sometimes he needed a push thanks to his bad habit of procrastination. It was a typical Monday morning in the church office. The church treasurer had dropped off the visitor cards earlier, along with the special prayer request notes that members of the congregation had dropped in the offering plate.

"I organized the prayer requests and put them on your desk. You need to make some phone calls to answer some of them. Or maybe you could email. It doesn't much matter, does it? You just need to get them done."

Blast it! He didn't need to be told every little thing to do. He thought about making a flippant remark, but didn't. She really did have his back and without her, he wouldn't be nearly as efficient or organized. If she would just quit acting like a mother hen!

Then he admonished himself. You really do need a vacation, old boy! She does this every week and it hasn't bothered you before! You need a mother hen and you just don't want to admit it.

"Thanks Reva, I'll get to them in just a few minutes. And yes, I have found someone to fill in while I'm gone. I have his file in my desk drawer. I should have already given it to you by now."

He would be gone for two back to back Sundays. Reva had overheard him and Liz chatting in Rock's office one afternoon. Wouldn't it be nice, Liz had said, if they could have a few days by themselves before the rest of the family arrived for the week? Reva whispered in a few ears. Meanwhile, the Session got wind of it and insisted that he take off two Sundays instead of one, giving them a chance to go down a few days early.

The Clark clan had arranged to rent two large houses less than a block away from Miss Edie's cottage. Rock was glad to see that Liz seemed to be genuinely thrilled with the idea of spending a week with them. He hoped she wouldn't be sick and tired of them before the week was up. He knew she could handle his immediate family - his parents, two sisters and their families, but his uncles and their families were a different story. Two of them were preachers and both had greatly influenced his decision to go into the ministry. His Uncle Mike's daughter, Jo Ann, had three children, stepping stones actually, and unless their behavior had greatly improved, they would make Liz question her sanity in ever wanting to have children. Add a couple of sulky teenagers that belonged to John and it should be an interesting vacation. His Uncle Joe, on the other hand, was a medical doctor. He had married while still in medical school. His young wife could never get used to the long hours through his residency, and had divorced him just three years into their marriage. He had never remarried, but now in his early sixties, had settled down in a relationship. He was quiet, but assertive and didn't hesitate to tell the others that he could only take them in small doses and he would be staying in a condo at the other end of the island. He and his friend would join them for dinner and socialize for a while, but then would escape to the peace and quiet of their own island getaway afterwards.

He was so glad he and Liz would have Miss Edie's beach cottage all to themselves. He was looking forward to some time alone with her with no demands from his congregation.

Finding someone to tend his flock while he was gone for eleven days had been easier than he thought. He felt he'd found the perfect person. Ned Jones was a recent graduate of seminary and was excited to get some experience. Not only could he fill the pulpit, but he offered to work in the church office and even do hospital visits if needed. Rock was impressed with the young man's enthusiasm. The session had just approved hiring a youth minister with funds the church had received through an estate gift and this was an opportune time to see if Ned would be a good fit for that position. It was amazing how God seemed to bring the right people into the path of those who needed them - like the way He had brought Liz into his life - and of course, Reva, his mother hen.

There was a short knock on the door. He looked up as Liz walked in. She greeted Reva warmly, reaching down to give her a hug.

"It sure is good to see you, Miss Liz. We never had any time to sit and talk a spell before you quit work. And I reckon it must be agreeing with you since you look so cheery and rested."

"Thank you, Reva. I didn't realize how much stress I was under at work until I left. I was glad to hand it over – especially the end of year testing!

Rock still couldn't get used to her being home in the middle of the day. "I was just thinking about you," he said.

"Good thoughts, I hope," she said.

"Always." He got up from his desk and gave her a kiss. "I love having you home. I was just thinking about running home for lunch."

"I'll go you one better," she said. "I made some picnic fixings so we can eat lunch on one of the benches in the courtyard. It's the warmest day we've had all Spring."

"Exactly what I was thinking," he said.

She laughed. "You were not thinking that!"

"Well I wish I had thought of it," he teased. "You always come up with the good ideas?"

"That's because I'm resourceful." She grabbed his hand. "The picnic basket is already out on the bench," she said. "Let's get out there before somebody comes by and steals it."

"Or the ants walk off with it." It wasn't a very original line, he knew, but his dear wife smiled anyway.

He looked at Reva apologetically.

"Go on," she said. "You can work on those prayer requests when you finish eating lunch with this dear girl."

He looked relieved and practically ran out the door, tugging Liz along behind him.

Reva shook her head and spoke to the door that had just closed in her face. "What would he do without me?"

CHAPTER 8

"*L* isten to advice and accept instruction, that you may gain wisdom in the future.*"

- Proverbs 19:20 ESV

Rock woke up with Theo sitting on his chest watching him. He looked over at Liz who was sleeping soundly. He got up quickly before Theo got wound up and woke her up. Theo had started coming in their bedroom at exactly 6:30 a.m. each day as if a programmed alarm clock went off in his head. He would meow for a while and if they ignored him, he would jump on the bedside table and start methodically knocking things off the table and on to the floor. He had already done all that this morning as Rock could see when he stood up and almost stepped on his reading glasses. Fixing the door handle on the laundry room door had just been bumped up to high priority status. When Jay Harvey had installed a new door from the kitchen to the laundry room during the kitchen remodel last Fall, the latch was just a touch too high for the latch plate. Although content to sleep in the laundry room at night, Theo was determined to push the door open when he wanted out in the morning.

He needed to be up anyway. Now that Liz wasn't working, he had started following his old routine of taking a fresh cup of coffee into his study to have a few quiet moments in prayer, then reading his devotional and Bible before he started his day.

He had left his appointment calendar at the office, but he knew he had a busy day ahead. He also needed to make a run to the post office. Liz had put a package by the door last night for him to mail so it would arrive in Marietta in time for his mom's birthday. He suggested they just wait and give it to her at the beach - it was only a couple of weeks until they would see her there, but Liz responded by giving him the evil eye, something he had not seen prior to their marriage. She was pretty good at it too, and it would have had more of an impact if she hadn't laughed hilariously at his expression when she did it.

After a quick shave and shower, he was ready. He had almost forgotten that Reva had told him before she left the office yesterday not to eat breakfast. When he asked why, she just smiled. "It's a secret," she'd said. He flew out the door with visions of her famous homemade cinnamon rolls in his head. He was not disappointed.

***

Liz called to tell him that she was driving to Rock Hill to run some errands and get her hair trimmed. "Don't forget our 4 o'clock appointment today for my ultrasound," she reminded him before she left.

"How could I forget?" he said. "It's all I can think about. Will you be back home so we can ride together or should I meet you there?"

"I'll be home by 2:30. We'll ride together."

Rock decided to forego lunch since he was already stuffed with cinnamon rolls, so he took off for the post office with the birthday package for his mom.

"Well, it's official Rev Rock! My retirement date is June 9th."

Rock's jaw dropped as he took in Betty's news. "You can't retire," he said. "What will happen to us?"

"You'll get you a new postal worker and you'll be just fine." Rock noticed that her smile had not made it all the way up to her eyes, and that was a surefire way to tell that their postmaster of thirty odd years was not completely happy with her decision. Sure, she had talked nonstop about retiring for the last six months, but no one expected that she really would.

"Betty! That's just a few weeks away," he said. "You're just up and leaving us high and dry." He stood there in confusion trying to imagine coming to the post office without Betty there to aggravate him. She was the glue that held the town together. She was the first to know when a fox got into Louise Ledford's chicken coop and killed all her laying hens. She was the one who called 911 when Lou Higgins had a heart attack mowing grass at the park. She rescued more dogs than the animal shelter. This was just so unexpected. But then he remembered all the little warning signs. She had started taking her personal things home. It was funny he hadn't noticed how empty the post office walls were. She had taken all her pictures down. Rats - she really was going to retire.

When he looked back up at her, her eyes were filled with tears, not yet spilling forth, and he understood. "You really don't want to retire, do you?

The dam broke and she sobbed. "I've made the wrong decision, Rev Rock. What am I going to do?"

Was he and all the other people in town being selfish wanting her to stay? He wondered if their disappointment had made her doubt her decision. Thirty years, here in the same tiny post office. "Betty, I'm sure you made the right decision. None of us want you to go, but we don't want to hold you back either. Think of all the fun things you can do."

She cried even louder. "But I don't want to do fun things. Y'all are my family. I can't think of a single thing I want to do, except maybe sleep late now and then."

Wanda Burns walked in the door. "What's wrong?" she asked when she saw Betty's tears. The dam broke again and Rock decided it was time to make his exit. It was too depressing. Tears always did him in. Then he remembered he had a package to mail.

"Aw, go on and get out of here, Rev Rock," Betty said through her sniffles. "I see that Liz printed the shipping label online. Go on before you see my eye makeup smeared." He got out while the gettin' was good.

***

He was sitting with a blank stare thinking about Betty's retirement when Kit and BJ Jones walked into his office at exactly 2:15, their scheduled appointment time. BJ's Diner opened for the breakfast and lunch crowds, staying sometimes half the afternoon, but today they had locked the doors at 2.

Rock gave Kit a hug and shook hands with BJ. "How's the Jones household adjusting to its two newest additions?" Rock asked.

It was a subject BJ loved to talk about. "It's different, all right. I don't know how we got so lucky. It's noisy with the two of them, but a good noisy, if you know what I mean."

Rock nodded. An amazing couple. Having lost their only daughter in a car accident a few years earlier, there had been a big hole in their hearts. A heart healer, in the form of Maria, a young pregnant Hispanic woman fleeing an abusive husband had brought new joy to their lives when they took her in when she had no place to go. Suddenly their household went from two to four when the baby was born right before Christmas.

"In other words, we're loving every minute of it," Kit said.

She and BJ were standing side by side, and Rock wondered how such a great big heart could be in this tiny little redhead standing in front of him. Right now the two of them were doing everything in their power to adopt Maria, so she wouldn't be forced to return to her native Honduras when her visa expired. "What is Maria doing now?" he asked.

"She's been taking some night courses at the community college to try to catch up. They're geared for students who want to get their GED, but she's not settling for that. We're hoping she can enroll in high school as a senior next year. She's smart, that one is! Her mother-in-law was right - she's a fast learner, soaking up knowledge like a little sponge. I think she can do it, even with the language barrier."

Rock laughed. "Language barrier? She speaks better English than a lot of American kids I know. Or maybe it's just because I don't understand their slang language."

Kit laughed with him. "I think they just don't want us old fogeys to understand what they're saying."

Rock opened the top drawer of his desk. "I have the letter of recommendation that you asked me to write," he said. "Bob Clayton told me Sunday that there are a few loopholes in the immigration policy that he's hoping to get around. He seems pretty sure they'll extend her visa while she's going to school."

"Thank you, Rev Rock." She took the letter from his hands. "This letter, along with the others we've got, will get the adoption process rolling and hopefully, the two of them will get to stay here permanently."

"We're claiming a miracle anyway," BJ said. "God hasn't let us down yet through this whole thing with Maria."

"We'd better get going," Kit said. "I want to get this to Bob's office before he closes." She reached up and gave Rock another hug. "Thanks again for everything. We appreciate all you've done. Oh, I forgot to ask – how's Liz doing?"

"We're going for another ultrasound today."

"Aw, I would love to be a fly on the wall and watch your face as you see that little baby again."

Rock watched them walk out the door and said a prayer that their hearts wouldn't be broken again.

***

Liz was quietly flipping through the December issue of Southern Living magazine while Rock was busy watching the other women coming in and out of the waiting room of Dr. Alexander's Ob/Gyn practice. He was trying to guess their due dates based on what he knew about pregnant women, which was not much. What he did know and love was that his beautiful wife was in her third trimester. He had been trying to keep up with the weeks – was this thirty-two or thirty-three? It was all so confusing. The door to the inner offices opened and he let out an audible gasp at the sight of the person walking out. Her stomach was huge - about the size of a beach ball, maybe bigger. He elbowed Liz and whispered, "Will you get that big?"

She looked up. She and the other woman exchanged smiles and she walked out the door. "I hope not," she said. "She's having twins and she's close to delivery time. We usually have appointments on the same day, but I don't think I'll be seeing her after today. She's carried them longer than they expected – it should be any day now."

"Twins, now that would be nice." He looked at her out of the corner of his eye and smiled. "Maybe next time?"

"Don't even think about it," she said. "You would get so excited, there would be no containing you. Remember how you acted when we had our first ultrasound. You jumped up and down when the technician told us it was a boy. The windows were shaking and I was embarrassed."

"I would have jumped up and down just as much if she'd said it was a girl." He reached over and brushed a strand of hair out of her eyes. "I was just excited that it was a baby, our baby that we were watching on the screen. The images were so clear."

"It was pretty amazing, wasn't it?" she said. "Now that he's growing, they'll be even clearer and his little facial features will be more defined." She held her hand over her stomach and waited. "He's been doing cartwheels all day and now he'll probably sleep right through the ultrasound. Here," she said, "put your hand right here."

She reached out and led his hand to the spot. There was no movement at all. "Uh, wouldn't you know it? Our boy has decided to be lazy."

"Our boy," he sighed, keeping his hand on her stomach for a while longer. "Do you know how happy you've made me, Liz?"

She looked at the man she had married and said a silent prayer of thanksgiving. "Yes, I think I do."

The door opened to the inner offices. "Mr. and Mrs Clark?" They both stood up at the same time. "I'm Cathy - Let's get you ready to take a look at this little fellow." She closed the door behind them and turned to Liz. "Do you have a full bladder?"

She and Rock looked at each other and laughed. "Always," they said in unison.

"Good, it needs to be full in order to get clear images. You two sit here while I get the examining room ready."

***

Liz picked up a New Parent magazine and started reading. Rock just sat there watching her. The last few months had flown by. After Christmas, they had gone first to visit Liz's family to break the news of her pregnancy. Liz was an only child and the Wagner's had already reconciled that they would never be grandparents because of Liz's inability to conceive during her marriage to Ron. Rock smiled when he thought back to Eleanor's reaction to their news. Eleanor's hobby was crocheting and she looked puzzled when she opened one of the Christmas presents they had brought. It was a set of crochet needles, some yarn and a pattern for baby booties. Rock was surprised at Liz's choice of gifts - Eleanor Wagner didn't seem to have a crochet kind of personality. He watched with amusement as she threw the package aside and jumped up and down like a madwoman. It was apparent that Liz had inherited her dad's more conservative personality, but Eleanor's excitement was contagious and he and Liz were overjoyed at her reaction.

Then it was time to visit the Clarks to share the news. Irene had insisted that she had suspected it during their Thanksgiving visit with Rock and Liz. "The pregnant glow," she explained, "you can see it every time." She insisted on doing the needle test to determine the gender of the baby. She had never missed yet, she told Liz. As she held the thread with the needle over Liz's left hand, the needle started doing its work. It started off looking as if it would go around in a circle, but then it straightened up and started going in a back and forth motion, a straight line. "It's a boy," she announced matter-of-factly, then realized what she'd said and yelled out to Will, "It's a boy, Will. Now you'll have a boy to carry on the Clark name."

"I don't give a hill of beans about the Clark name," Will said. "I'm just excited to see these two so happy and in love, whatever the gender may be." He got up from his recliner and shook Rock's hand, then took Liz's hand gently in his. "Thank you, Liz, for making our boy so happy. We love and cherish you just like a daughter." Rock could tell she was touched, and a few tears spilled over and landed on her cheek.

The tech came back and led them to the examining room. "I'm ready if you two are," she said.

"I'm ready to see who he looks like," Rock said.

"He'll look just like you," she teased, "even down to the crooked left ear."

He gave her a hand to get up on the examining table, then walked over to the mirror over the small sink. "My left ear isn't crooked," he said.

She laughed. "I knew you would have to look."

"Just lay back and get comfortable, Liz, and put this pillow under your head." Cathy fluffed and positioned the pillow. "Now, scoot up on the bed just a little - that's it." She stepped back and adjusted the screen. "We should be able to see the features quite well. This is your second ultrasound, isn't it?"

Liz rolled her eyes. "Oh yes, because of my age. This 'because of my age' thing is making me start to feel ancient. I'm glad to have the ultrasound though. I want to see him again."

The technician laughed. "You're younger than I am," she said. "And I'm still considering having one more." She picked up a large tube from the table. "This will be cold at first," she said as she spread a layer of gel over Liz's stomach.

As she rubbed the wand back forth, Rock watched in amazement. "Oh my stars," he said. "Liz, look! He's beautiful!"

"Boys are handsome, girls are beautiful," Liz said, laughing as she witnessed his excitement. She turned her head back to the screen. Her heart filled with love as she watched their little boy suck his thumb and then move the other tiny hand up over his head.

"A miracle," Rock said in awe as a whole new wave of emotions washed over him.

CHAPTER 9

"*E*verything they say is crooked and deceitful. They refuse to act wisely or do good.*"*

- Psalm 36:3 NLT2

May was a transitional time for the islanders. Most of the Canadians and northerners who wintered there had left nearly a month ago, and the vacation rental season had not yet begun. It was a good time of the year for the permanent residents. They had the beach to themselves, or almost, having to share it only with the seasonal homeowners who came down during April and May to ready their houses to be rented out again for the summer. The majority of the homes on the island were second homes. The owners could make enough money through summer rentals to tourists and winter rentals to the snowbirds to pay their mortgage payments for the entire year.

The west end of the island was quiet except for the few daily walkers searching the beach for shells. Peterson had been hard at work setting the stage for strange occurrences he had planned for the Devil's Footpath when the summer tourists arrived. He had already done a test run, trying his scare tactics on a few of the local residents. A simple white plastic bag being pulled by a cord had caught the attention of the Mosher lady as she walked on the beach. And he was sure she had seen the small fire he had set with one of those three-hour fire logs he had bought at Walmart. The marsh grass was tall and with the scrubby pines offering a good hiding place, it was going to be easy to carry this off.

He wasn't really worried about the old man keeping his secret. Not many people would pay attention to the scruffy old guy, but when strange things started happening, the old timers on the island would remember the stories of the Devil's Footpath and the spooky legends that went along with it. Some of them would recall another year, back in the 1950's when ghost stories abounded. It was a phenomenon that no one had ever been able to explain. Paranormal activity - that's what the archived copy of the Brunswick Beacon had called it. Some said it was the ghost of Blackbeard wandering the coast of the Carolinas, but others were sure it was the unsettled spirits of the Tuscarora Indians that had been captured and killed nearby by the British in the early 1700's. He didn't set any stock by either of the stories.

He would come and go by pulling his canoe into the little canal along the waterway so as not to attract attention from the beach side. All he wanted to do was scare the property owners and make them change their minds about selling their beach houses. It shouldn't be all that hard. The author who had stayed in the Mosher house last summer had already started the ball a'rolling with her book about the area. He just had to keep it going. The book had been published in late Fall and when the locals read it, there had been a throng of people hitting the west end of the beach to try to get a glimpse of a ghost or a bonfire. There was nothing to see so the rumors had died down, but now he planned to remedy that with tricks of his own. If a bonfire was what they wanted, he would oblige. If a ghost or two was needed or shadows and things that go bump in the night, he would figure out a way to do it. This should be fun. He would just have to be careful and not get caught.

Had he known the real story behind the strange goings-on around the Devil's Footpath last year, he wouldn't be so eager to be there alone. As he made his way back to his canoe, an involuntary chill came over him. He picked up his pace and talked aloud as if it would scare off any unwelcome visitors. Then he laughed gruffly and shook it off. "I'm doing such a good job, I'm spooking myself," he said, and got in the canoe and took off.

CHAPTER 10

"*L*et no one seek his own good, but the good of his neighbor."

- 1 Corinthians 10:24 ESV

Reva stared out the window as a shiny new SUV with a dealers license plate pulled into the parking lot. Holly was sitting at a small table folding the bulletins for Sunday's service. She had been serving as a volunteer in the church office since she, Sonny and Abby had moved out of the home of his parents and into the old parsonage after the restoration had been done. She had enjoyed living with Maura and Danny, her in-laws. They had shown her nothing but love and support during her recovery from the car accident last summer, but it was time for the young family to find a home of their own and the timing had been perfect. Just a short walk across the street, they were near enough to visit, but far enough away for privacy.

"Come look at this, Holly," Reva called. "Someone in town has a nice, new ride!"

Holly got up and walked to the window, just as a man opened the driver's side door and got out. "That's Rev Rock," she said.

"Lord a'mercy, it sure is," Reva said. "He finally sold that old truck! Lee Robinson's Garage is going to have to file bankruptcy without that truck to work on."

The office door opened and Rock walked in, greeted by two faces staring at him. "What?" he said, looking from one of them to the other.

"You know what," Reva said. "You sneaked a new car in here and didn't even tell me you were getting one."

Rock grinned. "It's the first time," he said. "You always know what I'm going to do before I do it!"

She nodded her head in agreement. "That's true. Don't much get by me. Has Miss Liz seen it?"

"Are you kidding me? I learned at least one thing from my Daddy. Don't ever buy something your wife doesn't know about. Even if she loves it, she'll be mad as a wet hen." He smiled, thinking of his parents. "Of course, he is married to the one and only Irene Clark."

"Well, your daddy was right. We women do like to have a say-so in it."

"We really didn't have much choice. My truck is a two-seater and Liz's car is a two door. It would be a little hard getting a baby in and out of it. We went car shopping last night. They cleaned it up this morning, so we drove to pick it up."

"It's nice," Holly said. "What kind is it?"

"It's a Ford Explorer," Rock said. "The old truck's a Ford, and it's been a good one." He looked out the window. "Liz will be home shortly - she had to stop by the drugstore."

"She drove your truck?" Reva looked incredulous.

"Heaven's no. She drove her car. The truck's in our garage."

"You mean you didn't trade it?"

"Trade it? I couldn't do that - we have too much history together. Everybody needs a truck."

"Hmph," Reva said. "It's just going to be an eyesore in our parking lot."

Rock rolled his eyes. "It won't be in our parking lot - it'll be in our garage. She's selling her car to..." He turned and pointed, "to Holly, here. Holly has been without a car since her accident last year and she needs something small for running Abby back and forth to school."

Reva turned to Holly. "You knew about this and didn't tell ol' Reva? Y'all let me ramble on and you both knew about it!"

Holly smiled. "No way am I getting in the middle of this one," she said. "I'm just minding my own business folding the bulletins."

Rock broke down and laughed, more at Reva standing there with her hands on her hips than anything else. "Good answer, Holly." He started back to his office. "Do I have any messages?"

Reva sighed, "You've got several phone messages," she said. "Everybody seems to be in a panic that you're going to be gone for two weeks. They're just dreamin' up stuff to ask you about before you go."

"I'll return the calls, but they needn't worry. Ned Jones will take good care of things while I'm gone."

"I know that - and you know that," she said. "We've just got to convince everyone else."

"I forgot how much trouble it is to go on vacation," he said, and started to shut the door.

"Wait!" Reva called out.

He stuck his head back out the door. "Did you forget something?" he asked.

"Yes, you told me to remind you to go to the post office before it closed today."

"Oops," he said. "I'd better do it right now before I forget. I need to sign something saying it's okay for you or Ned to pick up my mail while we're gone." He picked up his jacket again and started for the door.

"Don't expect me to pay your bills," she said as he opened the door to the outside.

"I've already taken care of that," he said. "They're automatically deducted from my bank account."

"Well, la de da," she said, and winked at Holly.

Rock turned around and gave her his arched eyebrow look. "I don't know why, but I'm going to miss your smart mouth while we're gone."

***

There was a line inside the Post Office when Rock walked in. He remembered the days just a couple of years before when you could walk into the post office almost any time of the day and be the only customer. And there had been no talk then of closing or reducing the hours of the post office. And now, even though business was booming since Sun's Up Retirement Village had started using the post office, they were going to reduce the business hours to half days. A town hall meeting had been held with representatives from Charlotte, but it didn't do any good - the decision had been made.

Hank Burns was at the counter and Betty was fussing. "You tell Wanda Burns that I am not her personal postmaster," she said. "She needs to learn how to wrap a package." She was using a large shipping tape dispenser to seal every corner while Hank held the box.

There was a woman in front of Rock, a new customer. Rock was amused when she gasped in horror. "Does she talk to everyone like this?" she asked him.

"No, only to those she loves," he said. "Her attitude is part of the charm that keeps people coming back in here. You'll love her when you get used to her."

She looked confused for a moment and then she smiled. "Oh, I get it. It's another one of those southern things, isn't it?" He nodded. She seemed very smug that she was finally beginning to understand the culture of the South.

Rock was the last person in line, and when everyone else had gone out the door, Betty was groaning. "This has been the busiest day ever!" she said, and let out a sigh.

"When are the new hours supposed to go in effect?" he asked.

"It was supposed to be June 1st, but they keep changing it. I had already posted it on the door, and now they call me and tell me to take it down, so in answer to your question, I have no idea."

"We're leaving out Thursday morning for vacation," he said. "I've written a note here giving permission for either Reva or Ned to pick up our personal mail along with the church mail."

"How long are you going to be gone?" she asked.

"Almost two weeks. We'll be back on June 6th."

"You'll miss my retirement party!"

"No, not that soon!"

"Yep, June 5th is my last day."

Rock's shoulders slumped. "It's probably a good thing we won't be here. I don't want people seeing me cry over you leaving." Big tears were rolling down Betty's cheeks.

"Uh, I've gotta get out of here," he said gruffly. "You better still be here when I get back." He turned around and hurried out the door determined to blink away any stray tears that might happen to make themselves stroll down his cheek. It couldn't be! With Betty gone, it will be the end of an era. Who else would care so much about the community? He knew in his heart that Betty deserved retirement, but for the life of him, he was having a hard time being happy about it. He knew one thing for sure; there would never be another Betty.

***

Rock looked at all the bags and boxes on the floor waiting to be taken out to the car. "Liz, honey. We don't need half this stuff. Miss Edie told me that the linens are on the beds, there are plenty of towels and she has a washer and dryer so we shouldn't need so many clothes." He picked up one of the bags. "Do you have a kitchen sink in here?"

"No, silly," she said. "That bag has canned foods. It's easier to go to the grocery store here than down at the beach. I don't want to waste a minute of our vacation time grocery shopping."

He laughed at her and pulled her close. "Neither do I. Especially these next few days by ourselves. Long romantic walks on the beach, afternoon naps, candlelight dinners on the porch, midnight skinny-dipping..."

She snuggled into his chest. "You're making me swoon, Reverend Clark. It's enough to make a preacher's wife blush." She pulled back and gave him a playful swat on the arm. "Now get a move on! I can't wait to get there."

CHAPTER 11

"L et him kiss me with the kisses of his mouth; For thy love is better than wine."

- Song of Solomon 1:2 ASV

"Does this remind you of anything?" Liz asked. The rocking chairs had been pulled out on the open deck that extended off the screen porch. She and Rock had synchronized their back and forth motion in the rockers without even thinking about it. A pitcher of iced tea sat on a small tripod style plank table, alongside two glasses, empty except for a few cubes of ice and a slice of spent lemon in each. There had been a comfortable silence between them as they listened to the melody of the waves washing upon the shore.

"It reminds me of our courting days," he said, "before we knew we were courting." He smiled sideways at Liz. "The same two people, but with a change of scenery." He studied Liz's face as she watched the seagulls skimming across the water, then dipping below the surface. He picked up his tea glass and swished the ice around in the bottom before downing the last few drops. He picked out the lemon slice and put it in his mouth, making a sour face. "Do you realize that it was a year ago this coming Monday that Holly had her accident? It happened a few days before the school year was over. It seems like I was over at your house every afternoon when you got off work and we would have our tea on the porch and chat about Holly and Abby."

Liz looked at him and smiled. "Yeah, and after a few weeks of sweet tea and porch rocking, you started growing on me."

"I felt it too, but I didn't want to rush things. I was afraid of losing our friendship, so I held back. But I think we can safely say that Holly's accident jump-started our feelings for each other."

"In my opinion, it took you way too long! You were this close, Buddyroe...," she held her thumb and forefinger about an inch apart, "to making me lose all patience with you."

"I realized it too," he said, laughing. "That's why I took off like a scalded dog up the mountain pass to find you and propose to you before I let you get away." He set his glass back on the table and reached over to take her hand. He rubbed his thumb over the back of her knuckles. "I love you, Liz." He got up from the rocker and pulled her up from her chair. "We've already taken a long walk on the beach this morning, I've caught enough fish for our supper, it's too cold for a swim, so how about we take a nap?" He looked at her and raised an eyebrow. She giggled and walked ahead of him. "Last one in bed gets the flat pillow!"

In Liz's opinion it had been a perfect day. They had taken their beach chairs out to the surf after dinner and were now enjoying the last few rays of sun before it settled beyond the horizon. Edie had told her about the fabulous sunsets on the Brunswick Islands. The coastline practically made a U-turn at Southport turning sharply to the west instead of continuing its southward path. Because of this, the islands were south-facing beaches. It was amazing to think you could watch the sun rise over the ocean to the east and then see it set over the west corner of the ocean in the evenings, therefore making for awe inspiring sunrises and sunsets every single day. She and Rock held hands and watched the flaming rays settle down beneath the surface of the sea.

As the day came to an end, they went back in and settled on the sofa snuggling up in a blanket side by side. Rock filled her in on the many personalities of the Clark family, his uncles and their wives, his cousins, and his nieces and nephews. They talked of baby names.

"Eli," she said.

"Matthew," he said.

"Rockford."

"No! Not Rockford - poor kid will have the same trouble with nicknames I've had." They both laughed.

"We have plenty of time to decide."

"I don't know - the time's going by in a blur."

They talked of mundane things and commented that it was rather nice not to have the phone ringing with questions, concerns and illnesses from his church members. Pretty soon Liz started yawning and they decided to go to bed early. Rock lay down in bed while Liz hit the shower, fully intending to shower after she finished. She brushed her teeth, flossed, then sat on the side of the bed applying body lotion to her slightly sun-tanned skin. "Aren't you going to take your shower?" she asked. He didn't answer. "Rock, Honey." He still didn't answer. She turned around and saw that he had fallen sound asleep. "I suppose that answers my question," she said as she got up from the bed. Now she wasn't sleepy at all.

She went to the kitchen and took a bottled water from the refrigerator, then walked from room to room looking at all the little touches that told of the happy moments the Mosher family had spent in the beach house. Baskets of shells picked up from the beach, a collection of lighthouses placed here and there throughout the house, and frames holding vacation photos of John, Edie and Paul and later ones of Paul, his wife and children. Some were taken on a boat and some were taken on the beach, showing laughing kids and adults playing in the surf. She wandered on into the library. Hundreds of books lined the shelves. John must have been a man of many interests. One shelf held a collection of historical books on the subject of World War II. Another held nautical books. Picking up a book about yachting, she wondered if he had ever taken up that hobby. Some were about fishing, knot tying and a thick mapbook titled *Navigating the Intracoastal Waterway*. She sat in the recliner for a moment and thumbed through the mapbook. Finally, she was getting sleepy again. She put it back on the bookshelf and walked over to the window facing the waterway. As she reached up to close the blind, she noticed what appeared to be a campfire burning out in the marsh. "That's strange," she said out loud, but then shrugged and carefully lowered the blinds. She yawned and thought no more about it and went to bed to join her sleeping husband who looked as if he didn't have a care in the world.

She gave him a kiss on the cheek. "Night, night, sleepyhead," she said to the man who had stolen her heart. She turned over and was asleep before it was time to turn the pillow over to the cooler side.

CHAPTER 12

"For the whole law is fulfilled in one word, even in this: Thou shalt love thy neighbor as thyself."

- Galatians 5:14 KJV

A sound he was not accustomed to hearing awakened him from a deep sleep. After a moment's confusion of his strange surroundings, he looked at Liz sleeping peacefully beside him and remembered that he was at the beach house. Excited to start the new day, he realized that as long as Liz was with him, he would be happy just about anywhere. The odd sound was there again. "A rooster - why is there a rooster at the beach?" he said groggily to himself as he made his way to the bathroom. He turned back and looked at the alarm clock by the bed. "And why start crowing at 5:30 a.m.? The sun's not even up yet." He looked in the bathroom mirror. "And why are you talking to yourself?" he said to the man with the day old stubble looking back at him. He felt along his jawline and looked for any bare spots. After seeing none, he wondered if he should grow a beard while he was on vacation. He looked back at his sleeping wife. Nah, no point in subjecting her soft, smooth face to a scratchy stubble over the next few days. He didn't want anything interfering with his favorite pastime, kissing and cuddling with his wife. He had a lot of kissing to do to make up for so many years with so few. He quickly lathered his face and got out his razor before he changed his mind. All thoughts of a beard were long gone after his shower.

As he measured the coffee grounds into the filter of the coffee maker, he noticed that the sky had turned from dark to a pale gray and wondered what time the sun would rise. He wanted Liz to watch it with him. Their first sunrise at the beach together – last night had been their first sunset. There were so many firsts that they had experienced together and he never took them for granted. Just thinking of spending every moment with her for the next ten days made his heart sing. It was true what they said about falling in love later in life. You realize what you've been missing and cherish each moment together. In your early twenties, you just assume that you'll meet someone and fall in love, but the odds get a little lower with each passing year. Who is this strange person talking about love, he thought, and chuckled. Last year at this time, he would have laughed someone out of the country if they had told him he would fall in love, get married and be about to become a father, all in just one measly year.

Miss Edie had warned Rock and Liz about her neighbor popping in and out and sure enough, Charlie knocked on the door just as soon as they'd finished eating their breakfast consisting of oatmeal and fresh strawberries.

"Aha," he said as he looked at the dishes on the table. "Y'all are early risers - well, you can have these eggs for breakfast tomorrow morning." He handed Liz an egg carton and she walked it over to the fridge.

"Wow," she said. "Thanks - I bought groceries before we left home, but didn't get many perishables. We planned to go today and pick up a few things."

"They're from my chickens," he said. "They lay more eggs than we can eat. And then there's the rooster." He sighed.

"Aha," Rock said. "I thought I heard a rooster this morning, but I said, surely not - not here on the beach."

"He was supposed to be a hen," he said.

Rock laughed. "I see he didn't make it." He pointed to an empty kitchen chair. "Have a seat and I'll get you a cup of coffee. Cream and sugar?"

"Yes, both." He stirred his coffee and sat back in his chair. "Back to the rooster - it was the funniest thing. Macie had ordered twelve hen chicks from Cackle Hatchery, and I never paid much attention to them. She was the one feeding and watering them out in their little house and chicken run. When they were about six months old, we started getting an egg here and there, and finally we were getting eleven eggs a day. Macie was bound and determined to find out which one wasn't laying and one day she came in and said, 'I think it's that funny looking chicken with the long tail. I've seen every chicken go into the house today except her.' I went out to see what all the fuss was about and lo and behold, that hen started crowing. You've got yourself a rooster, I told her, and I promise he's not going to lay any eggs. And you know what she said to me?"

Rock could no longer control his laughter, and Liz was no help at all. She had sat back down at the table and was laughing so hard she was snorting. "No, but please tell us," he managed to get out.

"Well sir, she said to me just as serious as a heart attack, 'A rooster! Well, he sure doesn't know how to treat the ladies. He's always jumping on their backs and scratching them'." He paused for effect, knowing that he was entertaining them. "You know, she and that writer lady..., Wanda, isn't it? They were like two peas in a pod. I'd have to leave the house when they got together. I was scared to death that whatever they had would rub off on me."

Liz had finally composed herself. "Charlie, I would love to meet Macie. If she's anything like Wanda, I know I would like her."

Charlie looked more serious and said, "We've lost two chickens in the last week, though. Macie's so attached to 'em. She's named every one of them. It was Princess and Rosemary who disappeared. It must have been a fox or a raccoon. There are more predators than you realize here on the island. We've even seen a possum." He paused. "Although, for the life of me, I can't figure out how they're getting in and out of the fence - especially carrying these fat hens."

"Oh," Liz said. "Please tell Macie I'm so sorry she lost her pets." We'll be on the lookout for wild animals while we're here."

Rock watched as the two of them talked. He liked Charlie already. He would be a fun neighbor to be around. Of course, he might have to talk to him about coming over unannounced for the next couple of days, but with a wink and a grin, he knew Charlie would understand. He was loving his alone time with Liz.

***

Liz was standing on the deck at the back of the house that overlooked the marsh grass and the Intracoastal Waterway when Rock walked outside to join her. "Beautiful, isn't it?"

She nodded. "That's a lot of land out there that's not being used. Why don't they build houses on it? Not that I think they should, but they seem to have built them everywhere else on the island."

"It's marshy and wet, I suppose," he said. "It's a good thing - they need to keep some of the natural habitat on the island for birds and small mammals. And deer too," he said. "I saw deer tracks when I took my short walk before breakfast. Their hoof prints were on the sand at the beach leading up to the sand dunes. I didn't try to follow them."

"Yes, and even foxes and raccoons roam the island according to Charlie." Liz looked out over the area behind the dunes. "It's so thick and scrubby back there, I don't know how they get through it."

"Deer love thick and scrubby. It makes a good hiding place from all the people."

"How would a person get through all that?" she asked.

"It would be about impossible," he said, "unless there's a path through there, and from up here, I don't see any signs of a path. Why do you ask?"

"I don't know. I saw a fire out in the middle of all that last night," she said, pointing her arm in a wide semi-circle that took in the whole area.

"A fire? Really? That can't be a good thing." He was thinking about his conversation with Miss Edie.

***

"Long walks on the beach and afternoon naps - this is the life." Liz looked at the waves as they crept closer and closer to the dunes. It was almost high tide. They sat on the two lightweight chairs they had pulled out from Edie's storage room in the carport on the ground level.

They had found a large thermos pitcher in the cabinet and filled it with sweet tea to refill their insulated clear plastic mugs. "We need to keep hydrated," Rock explained when Liz questioned why he needed the pitcher when they already had the large mugs.

"Ha, you're just addicted to tea," she said. "I'll bet you haven't even realized we've switched to decaf."

"So that's why it's not giving me my normal boost of energy!" he said. "And that's why I've been drinking more, thinking that it would kick in if I just drank enough."

"It's better for you," she said, "and for me since I'm not supposed to drink much caffeine." She looked out at the soft waves coming in closer with each push. "This is so nice. You're going to be all rested up when we get back to Park Place."

Rock's raised eyebrow and his wry grin told a different story. "If it was that simple," he said. "Just wait until tomorrow when the whole family gets here. I'm always more exhausted after vacation from trying to keep up with the kids. They think their Uncle Rock is their beach buddy, but of course it's my fault. Not having kids of my own, I've been their willing playmate - encouraged it even."

Liz laughed. "Well, I don't mind sharing. Tell me a little about your uncles. Didn't you say one of them has teenagers? He must be a good bit younger than your dad."

"John is Dad's baby brother - he's not but two years older than me. I call him John instead of Uncle John - calling him uncle just doesn't feel right. He's the one with teenagers. Lori is seventeen and Zach is eighteen. Lori will be a high school senior and Zach just graduated. He'll be off to Savannah State this fall, majoring in Marine Biology.

"And actually, Lori and Zach call me Uncle Rock, even though I'm their cousin. John encourages it because he thinks it's disrespectful for them to call me by my first name since I'm so much older."

"There's a twenty year spread in Dad, the oldest and John, the youngest. Mike is two years younger than Dad and Joe is somewhere in between - about ten years younger than Mike, I think. Grandma Clark had two miscarriages after Joe was born. Dad said it was hard on her, so she just gave up on having babies. Then John was born when she was in her early forties and Grandpa was forty six. Imagine their shock having another baby at that age."

"Just the same age as you."

He looked at her in surprise. "Well, when you put it that way.... I'm a fine one to be talking, huh? I've grown up with everybody telling me how old Grandma and Grandpa were when they had John, and here I am about the same age! But I don't feel old." He looked at Liz with a worried expression. "Do I look old?"

Liz reached over and took his hand. "You're the most handsome man I've ever met," she said. "Do you think all those mothers in Park Place would have been trying to fix up their twenty-something year old daughters with you if you looked old?"

He looked relieved. "I just don't want our little boy to be ashamed that I look more like a grandfather than a father."

"Rock, don't dwell on your age. No one else does and our baby certainly won't. He'll be the luckiest kid around to have a dad like you. It's all in how old you act, not how old you are." She let go of his hand and reached up and turned his head to face hers. "Just remember, God chose YOU to be a father to this child. Just trust Him. He knows what He's doing."

He put his arms around her. "You're wise beyond your years, Liz. Thank you for reminding me of that. I'm good at telling everyone else to trust Him, and here I am, questioning the most miraculous thing that's ever happened in my life. You're right, I promise I won't bring up the subject of age again."

Liz laughed. "Good! I'm getting tired of reassuring you. But of course, you could play the age card if you're smart. You said the kids like playing with you on the beach - I'll bet you could convince the teens to give you a break from playing with the little ones from time to time. Aching backs are good excuses."

"Good idea." He hunched over and grimaced for practice. "Oh, my poor aching back." He straightened back up and flexed his shoulders. "The bad thing is, I don't have to pretend. My back has been hurting ever since I had to carry the two dozen suitcases and boxes you brought to the beach."

She pinched his cheek. "Poor baby. I'm glad you finally grew up and got married."

CHAPTER 13

"And he said to them, *"Take care, and be on your
guard against all covetousness, for one's life does
not consist in the abundance of his possessions."*

- Luke 12:15 ESV

Peterson had seen all the cars come in on Sunday
afternoon from his vantage point inside the gazebo that
had been built as a common area for the residents of
Pelican Pointe. The beach was empty, but in his
sweatpants and windbreaker, no one would pay any
attention to him anyway. It was common for beach
walkers and runners to sit inside the shade of the gazebo
and take a break from the sun.

Four vans and a car had come, one right after the
other, and their occupants had unloaded suitcases and
bags of groceries into the two large beach houses. He
would have to check with the realtor and see how long
they would be there. He hadn't counted on such a crowd
- he hoped they wouldn't spoil his plans. With so many
people on the beach, it would be harder to come and go
through the footpath without being seen. Thatcher Realty
handled the rentals on most of the island's west end. His
own little real estate company was small potatoes
compared to Mark Thatcher's. Most of his own business
was selling the mobile homes and vacant lots on the
mainland. None of the major real estate companies
would touch them with a ten foot pole.

He wondered who could afford to buy those big houses, but then remembered that the owners rented out the huge mcmansions for exorbitant rates during the summer months. It was still considered off-season, but the biggest of the two houses rented for $10,000 per week during peak season. The summer and fall rentals would probably be enough to make the mortgage payments all year round. It took money to make money and he stayed on the edge of broke all the time. He wasn't interested in those houses though. He was after the two older cottages that had been built over fifty years ago. The Mosher house, the one that a man and his wife had been staying in the last few days, and the other one beside it owned by the older couple who lived here year round, Charlie and Macie McCann. If he could pull off buying those two houses, he could turn around and make a huge profit by reselling them to the construction company whose plans were to build up the marshy area behind them for a future development. The lots those houses were sitting on would be the only beach access for the development. The development couldn't be started without them. Jimmy Hodge had been trying to buy them, but he was on the up and up – he was above using scare tactics. Now if he could buy them and turn around and sell them to Jimmy, he could make a killing! The West End Resort gated community controlled all the other beach access and they weren't about to let theirs go. He smiled as he thought about island living and all the perks it would bring. Each time he met a pretty girl, she backed off when he brought her back to his place. A nice beach house would be a far cry from his manufactured home. Sure, it was in a nice neighborhood with plenty of trees and a mix of older and newer homes, but it wasn't a real house. The girl with the red hair, Renee it was, had told him so. She broke up with him after her first visit, but she would be begging him to take her back when he bought a place on the island. The thought pleased him.

He started back to his car. He wouldn't go to the trouble to build a fire tonight. The couple in the end house seemed to be connected with the newcomers. They had walked over as soon as the first van pulled in. There would be so much activity going on, they wouldn't notice anyway. He would take a break tonight and think things through. All sorts of plans were going on in the back of his mind as he thought about the old folks he was about to dupe. But one thing he hadn't counted on - they might be older, but they were much wiser.

***

Three dark figures stood in the middle of the circle at the end of the footpath. "Someone's been here." It was an observation, followed by profanity. Ove held a sack in his hand and a noise came from inside it. "They've built a fire, Tess. I think someone's trying to take over your spot. Where's the altar?" Ove was not his real name. Tess had given it to him when she had recruited him. It was a Viking name which meant 'full of terror', and she said it would fit him if he tried a little harder. He smiled too much – she needed to work on that.

"You know I wouldn't leave it out here for someone to find. I took it apart in December when I left. I hid pieces of it here and there under the scrubby pines so no one would find it."

The youngest of the three piped in. He looked to be no older than sixteen. Tess called him Geir, meaning 'man with a spear' because of the large machete knife he carried around. "No one oughten' to be out here anyways. It's impossible to find."

"We found it, didn't we?"

Ove was looking at the remnants of the fire. "They've used fire logs - looks like it was done recently. Must have been some kids come in by boat. It doesn't look like the path has been used since the last time we were here."

Geir was bringing a load of firewood from the direction of the path. "I cut enough with my machete for a good fire. I tried not to disturb things much like you said."

Tess spoke. "If we clear out too much, the path will be found by people walking on the beach, or people looking from the direction of the houses. We want to keep our sessions private like we did before."

The wood was piled high and the altar was put together. It was more of a small rustic table rather than a real alter. Its legs were easy to disassemble so they could hide it when they weren't around. One flick of a match and the flames came to life. Tess opened the sack and the sound of a squawking chicken was heard over the sound of the roaring fire.

A chanting and waving of arms indicted that the service had begun.

CHAPTER 14

"*In whose hand is the life of every living thing, and the breath of all mankind?*"

- Job 12:10 NASV

Liz had never witnessed such mayhem. All she could do was to sit back and watch as Rock's gregarious family tried to outtalk one another. She was an only child and her family gatherings had all been quiet and simple. She had aunts and uncles but they were spread out and rarely got together as a family anymore. Her first husband, Ron, had a large family but they never had extended family gatherings - only his brothers and sisters at Christmas, which was nothing like this. Even Rock was getting all caught up in their madness. The family had arrived after lunch, unpacked and invited Rock and Liz over for take-out pizza for dinner. All had gone well while they had their mouths full of pizza, but when they finished, it became a madhouse.

She got up from her seat hoping to go unnoticed into the kitchen. She needed to get out of here before she developed a headache, or worse, a panic attack. She opened the cabinet door over the sink and reached up high for a small glass for some water.

"Here, let me help you with that. These cabinets are tall." It was Rock's brother-in-law, Robert. He handed her the glass. "Do you want water or a soda?" he asked.

"Water's fine," she answered. "I felt a headache coming on."

He laughed, knowing exactly what she meant without her having to explain. "You can only take them in small doses until you get used to them. On my first vacation with Lisa and the family, my first thought was to get the heck out of Dodge, but after a few days, you adjust." He sat on a bar stool and pulled one out for her. "I still haven't found my voice when they're all together. The best thing to do is to sit back and observe. If you say something, odds are that they won't hear you anyway. You'll find them very entertaining after a while."

She felt a flood of relief. "I'm glad to hear that," she said. "It's good to know that I won't be pressured to add anything to the conversation. I honestly couldn't even gather my thoughts while I was in there."

"I know what you mean. Sometimes I think I could disappear for hours and they'd never know I was gone."

The thought of the family not even missing him made her chuckle. "That's good to know. Maybe I'll just go home and go to bed and see when and if Rock misses me."

"That wouldn't work with you," Robert said. "I've seen how protective he is of you. He can't take his eyes off you for very long. You wouldn't be gone ten minutes before he would put out a search party."

"Hmm.. I'm not so sure about that."

Just then, Rock walked through the kitchen door. "There you are! I wondered where you ran off to."

Robert laughed, "Speak of the devil." He got up from the stool and patted Liz on the shoulder. "She didn't run far. I think my new sister-in-law needed some fresh air, and that's not such a bad idea. Why don't we walk out on the deck and look at the moon. It's almost full tonight."

Rock and Liz followed him with Rock's hand placed firmly around her shoulder. He reached his head down to hers and blew gently on her neck. She shivered at his touch and leaned on his shoulder. This is what it's all about. I'm his wife and he loves me. I can handle his family for a couple of weeks out of the year, especially when I'm over the hormonal swings of pregnancy. She felt the self-pity she had been feeling lift away and knew she would grow to love his family.

The sky was free of clouds and the constellations seemed to stand out with all their clarity. The moon made the ocean waves appear to be edged in silver as they lapped upon the shore. The deck of the huge house was built close to twenty feet out and almost circled the house. Robert walked to the other side. Rock and Liz followed so they could get a clear view of the waterway and marsh. A cool breeze was blowing in from the west, and Rock wrapped his arms around Liz to keep her warm as she stood in front of him.

Robert continued around the deck, but stopped and pointed. "What's that!" he said.

They looked in the direction he was pointing and Liz was the first to speak. "That's what I saw the other night," she said. "It's a fire out in the middle of the marsh, except it wasn't so big then."

As they watched, the fire flamed a little higher and then was obscured as if something or someone was blocking it out. Just then they heard voices from the deck above them. The teenagers had come out on the deck and were exclaiming to themselves about the fire. They leaned out over the rails and called down to them. "Do you see what we see?" Zackary said. "It's creepy," chimed in his sister. The four of them scrambled down the steps and came to stand beside the adults. "What do you think it is, Uncle Rock?"

"I don't know," Rock answered. "But it is creepy. Maybe we can go exploring tomorrow."

"Why wait until tomorrow?" Zack's friend replied. "Let's go tonight. How about it Zach?"

"I don't think you would get very far tonight," Rock said. "It's a mess of briars and bramble bushes back in there. Let's wait until tomorrow."

"Okay, then. How about bright and early? 7 o'clock maybe?"

"Sure," Rock said, knowing full well from past experience that they wouldn't be out of bed until almost noon.

"You can count me out." Liz said.

"Ah, where's your spirit of adventure," Rock said, teasingly.

"It has nothing to do with spirit of adventure," she said back to him. "It's my spirit of common sense."

CHAPTER 15

"*C*hildren *are a gift from the Lord; They are a reward from him.*"

- Psalm 127:3 NLT

The sound of someone knocking on the back door caused Rock to sit up straight in bed. The knocking, however irritating, was welcome. It was a relief to be awakened from a nightmare where he was dreaming that his hands and feet were tied and he was sitting in front of a campfire watching in horror as devils with three-pronged pitchforks danced in the flames. "I'm coming," he shouted, as he grabbed on his pajama bottoms and headed with bare feet across the house until he reached the door and opened it. There stood four fresh faced kids looking at him expectantly. "What time is it?" he said, yawning.

"It's 7:15," Zack said. "I'm sorry we're late. Jake wouldn't get out of bed."

"Come on in, then." They followed Rock into the kitchen and sat down at the table. He yawned again and rubbed his eyes as he made his way over to the coffee pot. "Just let me put some coffee on. Do any of you drink coffee?"

"I do!" It was Lori's friend, Chloe. "I'll take cream and sugar if you have it."

He poured the water in and was grateful that Liz had measured everything out before they went to bed. "It's a

Bunn so it won't take but a minute. I'll be right back. I need to check to see if we woke Liz up." He left the room and went back to the bedroom. Liz was still asleep. He didn't know how she slept through all the racket. He hurriedly brushed his teeth and changed into his jeans and a long sleeve shirt. He reached for his sandals, but changed his mind and put on his tennis shoes. When he walked back into the kitchen, the kids were pouring orange juice and four frozen waffles popped out of the toaster at the same time. "Make yourself at home," he teased.

"We sort of did," said Lori, with a sheepish grin. "Where's your syrup?"

"In the cabinet over the stove," he said, pouring himself a cup of coffee. "What time did y'all get up?"

"6:30." Chloe was putting the cream back in the refrigerator. "We all set our alarm clocks. All except Jake, that is. We almost left without him," she said, popping him on the shoulder.

"That would have been fine," he said. "Our first day of vacation and y'all get up with the birds." He rested his head on the table while the others chatted excitedly.

"I'm with you Jake," Rock said. "I had no idea you would really be here at 7."

"7:15," Chloe mumbled, as she took her last bite of waffle.

"Whatever," he said, and grabbed himself a Pop-tart.

"Let's get going," Zack said and picked up his knapsack.

"Not so fast," Rock said, playfully pulling on the straps of Zack's knapsack. "Clean up the mess you made - don't leave it for Liz to do."

They made short work of cleaning up the kitchen and were out the door in five minutes. Rock left Liz a note, *Gone with the kids down the beach on a sleuthing adventure*, and taped it to the coffee pot. He put on his Atlanta Braves baseball cap and closed the door behind him.

***

Liz kept dozing off in her beach chair. She kept looking for the Clarks to show up on the beach, but she guessed they decided to sleep in late on the first day of their vacation. All except the teenagers who had gone with Rock for an adventure, he had said in his note. She was still not sleeping well. The baby had started moving around and kicking during the night and being calm during the day.

She had brought her journal out on the beach. She had been negligent about writing in it the last couple of weeks. Since she'd found out she was pregnant, she had tried to record all her emotions and milestones in the baby's growth inside her womb on a daily basis. The first month had been exciting and she had posted something every day, but now she was lucky if she remembered to post twice a week. She had just finished posting about her sleepless nights of late, when she heard a rush of activity behind her. The whole Clark clan was heading her way, with Lisa's children running up ahead, followed closely by Uncle Mike's grandchildren.

Rock's nieces and nephews, Gillian, Chase and Rachel were full of themselves. They didn't stop until they got to the water, then dipped their toes in and made their way back to Liz.

"Aunt Liz, did you miss us?" It was Rachel speaking. She was wearing a pretty pink and white sundress and a pair of pink sandals. Her blonde hair was pulled back in a ponytail, and Liz thought she was the prettiest child she'd ever seen. The children were all beautiful, but there was something about Rachel's aquamarine blue eyes that were remarkable. She wondered about the color of their own baby's hair and eyes. That was one thing you couldn't see in an ultrasound.

"Of course, I missed you," she said, pulling the child up into her lap.

Rachel patted Liz's stomach. "Is this where our baby cousin is living right now?" she asked.

Liz laughed. "Yes, I'm afraid he has some tight living quarters. I'm sure he's anxious to get out."

"It's a boy, isn't it?, she asked. "Why couldn't we have another girl?"

"For the same reason Chase wasn't a girl," she answered, pointing to Rachel's cousin, Chase. "You love him, don't you?"

Rachel thought for a while. "Yes, I do love him, but I'd rather trade him in for a girl."

"Hey, that's not fair"! Chase put his hands on his hips and poked his lip out in a pout.

"Chase, the odds are going to be a little more in your favor in a few weeks. You'll have another boy to play with when he gets a little older. And if he's anything like you, he'll be one lucky kid."

"Ha ha," he said, and poked his tongue out at Rachel.

"Sibling rivalry," Lisa said as she put her chair beside Liz's. "They're together so much, they act like sister and brother more than they do cousins." She looked at Liz. "You're getting a little pink - do you need some sunscreen," she said, handling Liz the bottle.

Liz took it. "Just on my face," she said. "I sprayed it on thick everywhere else, but I had a hat on when I came out. The wind picked it up and blew it clear across the dunes and I didn't feel like waddling over and picking it up."

"I know just how you feel," Lisa said. "I've been there. I'll get Robert to go over and find it after he plays in the water with the kids."

Will had pulled a cart loaded with beach chairs and he and Robert started setting them up. "Put mine beside Liz," Allison told her father.

"On the other side - I'm already parked on this side," Lisa said, while spreading out a beach blanket for the kids.

"I've got it!" Will said. "Let's just form a circle around Liz and we'll all be able to talk to her."

Liz wasn't quite sure how to take all the attention, but she laughed. "I've never felt so popular in my life, but how about we all go dip our feet in the water with the kids."

"I'll race ya!" Will said and started running.

"The turtle with the baby bump will be right behind you," Liz said, but easily outran her father-in-law.

CHAPTER 16

"*Do not be anxious about anything, but in everything by prayer and supplication with thanksgiving let your requests be made known to God.*"

- Philippians 4:6 NASV

Chase had found Liz's hat at the top of one of the dunes. She had it covering her face and was leaning back in her chair when Rock walked up with Rachel's beach bucket and poured water all over her feet. She shivered and pulled her chair up in a sitting position. She popped his leg with the journal she had on her lap. "Well, what did you find?"

"Nothing," Rock said, "unless you count these shells." He held up two almost perfect conch shells.

Zack had taken a seat in one of the empty chairs. "You forgot the weirdos walking on the beach."

Rock laughed. "I wouldn't go quite so far as to call them weirdos, but they were some interesting characters."

Chloe piped in. "No, Uncle Rock, you would have to call them weirdos. Nothing else fits. I, for one, am going to stay away from them. That girl had the grim reaper tattooed on her back and the boy had a tattoo of a snake wrapped around his arm. Creepy!"

Liz smiled. All the kids were now calling him Uncle Rock, even Zack and Lori's friends. "Were they really that bad?" Liz asked Rock.

"Bad enough that I would avoid them too," Rock said. "I don't like to be judgmental just because they have tattoos. Sonny is a perfect example of how I misjudged someone, but something about these kids made me feel uneasy, especially the girl. I'm calling them kids, but they're either late teens or early twenties."

"That seems like a kid to us," Liz said.

"I don't think they're staying around here. I watched them go to their car, which was parked near the now defunct gate. Maybe they just drove on the island to see the beach." Zack got up and Rock sat in the chair he had been occupying. "Where did everyone go?" he said, looking around.

"Uncle Mike took his crowd for a walk to the pier. I don't think they realize how far away the pier really is. They'll probably be calling us to pick them up. Your sisters and their husbands took the kids for a walk to pick up shells. There they come now," she said, pointing to the left.

"And look, the big kids are all in the water," Rock said.

"And your Mom and Dad were hungry so they went in to eat lunch. All accounted for," she said.

Rock looked to the right where John and his wife, Bonnie sat with their eyes tuned to the beach. "They're watching the kids," he said. "Let's go inside and eat lunch before anyone notices we're gone."

Liz jumped up and grabbed her towel. "Let's go. I'm hungry!"

"You're always hungry," he said, patting her on her belly.

"Last one in has to make lunch," she said, getting a head start and running on ahead. Rock let her get ahead. He didn't mind making lunch.

***

"What are our plans for tonight," Liz asked before she bit into her banana sandwich. "And by the way, this is a healthy lunch."

Rock laughed. "Well, at least we have a fruit and a vegetable on the menu."

"Where's the vegetable?" she said as she looked at the paper plate holding the sandwich, potato chips and a Little Debbie oatmeal cookie.

"The potatoes in the chips," he said.

"Oh, I feel much better now," she said. "Fruit, vegetables, and what's this?" she asked picking up her oatmeal cookie. "A whole grain! We are eating a balanced diet. And I'm sure the Duke's mayonnaise has its place somewhere in the food pyramid."

"I knew you would see the light," he said. "And about tonight - it's Uncle Mike and Aunt Gladys' night to fix dinner. Mom assigns each couple a night to fix dinner for everyone. I told her to put us near the end so we could see what everyone else is preparing so we'll know what to do when it's our turn."

"Good idea," she said. "I've got it - a Lowcountry chicken bog! It's easy and delicious. We'll have a salad to go along with it."

"Ah yes, that's what your mom had when we visited after Christmas. Chicken bog, it is."

After lunch, while Liz was taking a nap, Rock went into the library and pulled his email messages up on his laptop. Edie didn't have WiFi in the beach house, but Charlie and Macie gave him the password to theirs and he didn't have any trouble getting a connection. There were a few email messages and he made quick work responding to them. There was one from Ned Jones, asking his insight about a family who wanted him to counsel their fifteen year old daughter. He responded back with some background information and a reminder that when counseling, he should always leave the door partially open to Reva's office and to make sure Reva was in there. Ministers had to be careful or their reputations could be ruined with false accusations.

Reva had emailed him that he could view Sunday's bulletin on the church website, so he clicked over and found it. It seemed odd to see Ned's name beside 'sermon' and it almost made him homesick when he read the community announcements. A Memorial Day celebration at the park, the retirement party for Betty and a bridal shower for Beth Simmons on June 16th.

He sat there silently for a moment and prayed for his church family, for Ned as he prepared his next Sunday's sermon and for Betty with her mixed feelings about retirement. He went over his prayer list and spoke each individual by name.

When he finished his prayer, the day's events played out in his mind. He hadn't let on to Liz, but the two people's appearance and demeanor on the beach today had raised a red flag for him. He got back on his computer and googled CULTS. Page after page gave the names and practices of popular cults. As he looked through, he saw several satanic cults and a form of devil worshipping. The site showed some of the symbols and practices they use - pentagrams, serpents and swastikas to name a few. There was an image of a cult leader with tattoos covering his face and body. There it was! He enlarged the photo a little and could tell it was a grim reaper tattoo. It gave him chills to look at the flat and beady eyes of this cult leader in the photo, much like the chills he felt when he saw the girl this morning.

He heard Liz get up and close the bathroom door. He shut down the computer and closed his laptop. He didn't want to worry her with such disturbing images.

She came into the study to see him. "That little power nap was refreshing," she said. "Let's go back out on the beach. The kids are playing volleyball."

"Carry on without me," she yelled to the other players as she made her way back to her chair. She tired easily now and couldn't keep up the quick pace of the kids half her age. She watched Rock as he interacted with the teens. She was surprised at how well he kept up. In his shorts and t-shirt, he looked just as fit as the boys he was playing with. His habit of walking all over town, instead of driving all those years had paid off. She was just thinking how cute he looked when he turned around and smiled and winked. The irresistible rascal. He knows he's cute. She smiled and waved. "And I'm lucky enough to be married to him," she said out loud.

"What's that?" It was Allison putting her towel in the chair beside her. "Did I hear you say you were lucky to be married to my brother?" she teased.

"You did," Liz said. "Just don't tell him. He'll get a big head."

"Your secret's safe with me. But I think he's the lucky one. I've never seen him so happy. I've prayed so many times that he would find someone, but not just anyone. It had to be someone good enough for my big brother, and my prayers have come true. God had to be in on this - it's too perfect for anyone else to have planned it."

Liz was touched. "Thank you, Allison. I have no doubts that it was orchestrated by God. Falling in love again, our marriage and to top it off, my pregnancy in such a short period of time – it was a perfect plan for a life that has been so touched by sadness – a plan that I never dreamed was possible."

The volleyball game broke up and Rock and the kids walked over. "When's dinner," Zack said. "I'm starving!"

"That's what I came out to tell you," Allison said. "Dinner will be served at exactly 6 o'clock." She looked at her watch. "It's now 5:40, just enough time for you to all go clean up and get to the table. And all of you, grab as many of these chairs as you can hold. We're eating outside. Uncle Mike's grilling hamburgers and hotdogs."

Liz reached for some chairs and Rock stopped her. "You carry the light one," he said. "We'll get the rest."

Allison reached past Rock to get a chair. She sniffed the air. "Hmm, big brother. I think you volleyball players need to take a quick shower. The smell of freshly grilled hamburgers and sweaty armpits don't go very well together."

CHAPTER 17

"*B*ear *one another's burdens, and so fulfill the law of Christ.*"

- Galatians 6:2 ESV

Rock picked up his phone and examined the side button that switched it off and on. It was in the on position. He checked the volume and it was turned up high. It was already Tuesday morning and he hadn't received a single phone call. Most of his calls came in on the office phone, but the session members all had his cell phone number. So did Reva and Ned. Was there nothing happening in Park Place, or did they just not want to disturb him?

He scrolled through his contacts and found Ned's number, but then decided to call Reva at the office instead. She answered on the first ring. It was good to hear her voice.

"Reva, this is Rock."

"Who?" she answered. He'd only been gone five days and she acted like she didn't even know him.

"You know who I am." He decided to tease her a little. "The one who employs you!"

"Oh, that Rock," she said, and the deep, rich sound of her laughter echoed over the phone. "You've been gone so long I didn't recognize your voice. I hope you and Miss Liz are having a good vacation."

"We are. How's everyone in Park Place?" he asked. "Any news or problems in the church?"

"No, everything's just hunky-dorey. Oh, I forgot. My niece, you know Selma's youngest, had her a baby girl - eight pounds, four ounces with little peach fuzz hair. I went to see her in the hospital and got to hold her, yes I did. You know how crazy I am about babies."

Yes he did. Every baby that was brought through the church office doors found its way into Reva's arms. She could go on and on about babies so he'd better change the subject.

"How's Bruce Davis? Has he come home from the hospital yet?"

"Nope, they're not letting him come home yet. They're sending him to the rehab center in Lancaster for a couple of weeks. He's got to learn to walk all over again. I sure hope I don't ever break any bones. With this extra layer of fat on me, I couldn't hold myself up."

He never knew what to say when she brought up fat so he just ignored it. She might be a few pounds overweight, but he didn't think she was fat. Like his daddy once told him, "Rock, just plead the fifth amendment when a woman brings up her weight. You'll live longer."

"I'll give Bruce a call," he said.

"No need to. Ned's been visiting him every day."

"Good, good to hear that. Where is Ned? I'd like to speak with him a minute."

"He walked down to the post office. I was going to go, but Old Arthur has got my leg acting up, so he volunteered to go. I think Betty's got a crush on him."

Rock laughed. "Maybe that'll give the new preacher at Piney Ridge a break. Of course, I think he's been enjoying Betty's attention. He's a bachelor, you know."

"Now don't I know it. That's where my aunt goes to church and she says those single girls have been swooning over him. Tall, dark and handsome, that's what she says about him. But from what she's observed, our Betty does seem to have the inside corner on that market!"

"I've met him. He's a nice guy - just the kind Betty needs. Maybe he'll be the cure of her fascination for the bad boy type."

Reva laughed again. "She'd give up those bad boys in a heartbeat for a preacher. That's not even the church she goes to. She met him at a church conference back in January, but from what I hear, she's been visitin' there quite a bit lately." She paused for a minute. "When you comin' home? I hate to admit it, but it's no fun around here without you to aggravate."

"We should be home Sunday - late in the evening. Come Monday morning, you can aggravate me all you want, although I have enjoyed getting a reprieve from your insults."

"Do you want Ned to call you back?"

He hesitated. He was curious as to how Ned was handling things, but he didn't want him to think he wasn't confident in his abilities to carry on while he wasn't there. "No, just tell him to call if he needs me. And that goes for you too."

"Don't worry - we've got it covered." It made him feel good that they did.

***

After breakfast, Rock walked out the kitchen door to take the trash out. Charlie was checking the chicken wire on the fence he had built around the hen house. He had a puzzled expression on his face and walked from one end to the other as Rock was putting the bag of trash in the can.

"Anything wrong?" he asked, as he walked over to the fence to join him.

Charlie had his left arm crossed over his chest, holding his right elbow in his hand. His right hand was rubbing back and forth under his chin like he was in deep thought. He jumped when Rock spoke to him.

"Oh, you scared me. I was just trying to figure out how these varmints keep getting into my fence. There's no digging underneath and no broken places in the fence, but another chicken's missing. It's the tamest hen, Maggie. She's so tame, she'll let me pick her up, but she's never tried to get out." He looked up at the 6' tall fence. "And look, the netting on top is still there. The whole top isn't netted, just enough to keep a chicken hawk from swooping down and grabbing one. I keep their wings clipped so I know they can't be flying out the part that's not netted. Why, they can't even fly two feet off the ground, much less 6 feet." He put his arms down beside him and sighed. "And she was my favorite."

Rock felt sorry for him. He looked like he had lost his best friend. He walked over and put his arm on his shoulder. "How many have you lost now all together?"

"Maggie makes three. First there was Precious and Rosemary. That's going to cut down on our egg production - it's bad enough that we've lost three of our girls. The rooster has so far managed to evade whatever's getting them."

Rock hated to see him this way. "Is there anything you can do about it?" he asked, "like maybe buy one of those motion lights that come on when something comes near?"

"Well, I've been considering buying a motion camera anyway, and this has made up my mind. I think I'll run up to Walmart today and see if they have them. If not, I'll come back and get Macie and we'll ride down to North Myrtle. I know they have 'em at the Bass Pro Shop. Come to think of it, that's where we'll go. We'll make a morning of it and stop by Calabash to eat lunch on the way home. Macie likes to eat at the Seafood Hut."

Rock was glad to see that his mind had moved away from the missing hen, if only for the moment. "If you need any help putting it up, I'll give you a hand this afternoon."

"Sure thing," he said. "I'll go tell Macie to get ready. See you later."

He watched the older man as he walked up his back steps and into the house. He walked the fence line looking closely for any signs of animal tracks. There were the normal shoe prints in the sand - Charlie's, a woman's smaller shoe which must be Macie's and his own that he had just made as he walked about with Charlie. But there was another print - one that was particularly interesting. It was a smaller shoe than either he or Charlie wore, and it led off in the direction behind Edie's cottage and as he followed in the same direction, he saw that it went around the corner and over the dunes towards the beach. The sand on the dunes was so soft, there were just sunken in places and he couldn't see any more signs of the prints. He walked back not knowing what to think. There shouldn't be anyone walking so close to the house. He sure didn't like the idea of a stranger lurking around - especially a stranger who was a chicken thief.

CHAPTER 18

"*Be kind to one another, tenderhearted, forgiving one another, even as God in Christ forgave you.*"

- Ephesians 4:32 NKJV

He didn't want to scare Liz, so he didn't mention the chickens to her when he went back inside. The women had made plans to shop the local boutiques and gift shops as soon as they opened, so she had already dressed and was eating a bowl of cereal. The men had made plans to eat breakfast at the pier and then try their hand at fishing. Lori and Chloe were babysitting the smaller children with the help of the boys. John had given them firm instructions not to take them out on the beach. There were too many fast little feet to keep up with, so they would all be watching movies together.

The restaurant at the pier was almost empty. There were only two other people inside other than the cook and Molly, a waitress that they remembered from their last vacation. Two fishermen were sitting at the counter so they had their choice of tables. After the waitress took their order, Rock brought up the subject of the missing chickens. The others sat back and listened as Rock told them about his conversation with Charlie and about the shoe prints going around the house and onto the dunes.

"He had to pass right under our bedroom window," he said. "Too many odd things are happening - the fires, the theft of the chickens, the 'ghosts' that Charlie and others have seen - I can't help but wonder if the strange kids we saw on the beach have anything to do with it."

Will motioned for the waitress to bring him a coffee refill. As she refilled each of their cups, he spoke to her. "Thanks Molly. It's quiet here this morning. Where are all the fisherman?"

"It's a little early for tourists," she said. "Only the serious fishermen are out this time of year - shark fishing mostly."

"We're going to try our hand in a little bit. What's biting?"

She looked around the room, then whispered, "Well, to be honest, not much. Don't tell the pier owner I told you though. He would have my hide."

"How about on the surf?"

"You may catch a winter trout or maybe some whiting. The water probably hasn't warmed up enough for the flounder to come in yet."

"I did catch a couple of trout last week, Dad, so we should have some luck. Liz and I cooked them on the grill." He turned back to the waitress. "Let me ask you, Molly, we're staying on the west end of the beach between Pelican Pointe and the resort. Have there been any strange things going on down here this winter?"

"It's funny that you ask," she said. "Not this winter, but last summer, we had a rumor or two about ghost sightings along that end of the beach. Not that I put much stock in ghosts and such, but there was this writer who kind of got the rumor stirred up too. She wrote a book about it. Some of the gift shops down here carry the book and they can't keep it on their shelves."

Rock and his dad smiled and exchanged glances. "Wanda," Rock said.

"Yes, that was her name. You've heard of the book?"

"Yes, Wanda is a good friend," Rock said. "So nothing else happened?" he asked.

"Well, there were complaints about some of the permanent residents losing their cats, too. And a tourist lost one of those little Chihuahua dogs. My boyfriend worked part time for the police department last summer. He thinks some of the big owls on the island took off with them, because they disappeared without a trace."

"Hmm.. that's interesting," Rock said. "What part of the island?"

"All down near where you're staying." Molly looked up as two men walked in the restaurant and took a seat. "Y'all let me know if you need anything else. We've got some good fried apple pies for dessert. My mama made them this morning."

"I don't usually eat dessert at breakfast," John said. "But if I did, fried apple pies would be awfully tempting. I'll pass though." Everyone around the table nodded their heads in agreement, and Molly walked away to take the other patrons' order.

"Cats, a dog, and now chickens," Mike said. "Maybe the owls are getting the chickens too."

"I would have thought so, too," Rock said, "but Charlie has a cover made of netting over most of the fence just for that purpose. Even if they did get in, they would have a hard time getting out with a chicken in their talons. But owls really are a nuisance down here."

"Maybe we need to post guards," John said, winking at the others. "Mike you take the first shift tonight."

They all laughed. "I can just see that!" Will said. "Mike's always been sleep deprived. I'm surprised he doesn't fall asleep preaching his own sermons. He sure did his share of falling asleep in church when we were kids."

"Charlie's gone right now to buy a motion activated camera," Rock said. "But we do need to take this seriously. We have a lot of kids in our group. I think we need to be watchful. I don't want to ruin their vacation by scaring them all to death, though."

"I agree," Will said. "Irene would stay inside the whole time if she had an inkling there was something strange going on. Let's try to handle this ourselves. If we guys go anywhere as a group, one of us will stay behind keeping an eye out for things."

"Except, we won't leave Mike behind," John said. "He's liable to find the sofa much too comfortable." They paid up at the counter, and continued to rib Mike as they walked out of the restaurant. "Let's get on back," John said. "There's no one back there with the children except my teenage ragamuffins and their friends."

***

"Looks like Molly was wrong," Will said, as he and Rock started cleaning their catch for the day.

"Not bad!" Rock counted them. There were two redfish, four whiting, a pompano, and three flounder. "Maybe we'll catch more tomorrow and buy some shrimp so we can cook a seafood dinner one night." He looked around. "Where are the boys when we need them? It's time these younger kids learned how to clean fish."

"Oh, they know how, all right," Will said. "They just seem to disappear when the filet knives come out. They don't mind catching them - they just don't want to clean them."

"Here they come now," Rock said. "But I don't think they have fish cleaning on their minds. They're too dressed up for that."

The four teenagers came bounding down the stairs. They all stopped as soon as they reached the bottom. "You ask him," Zack said, looking at Lori.

"Huh uh! It was your idea."

Rock looked from one to the other. "Ask who what?"

"Can we borrow your new car to go play putt-putt?" Zack asked.

Rock smiled. "I don't have a new car. Liz has a new car. If I was driving my truck like I always do, I would gladly let you borrow it." He laughed. "But I think you would be asking somebody else to borrow their car since you all know what my old truck looks like. Liz would have my hide if I let you drive the Explorer. She doesn't have the new worn off it yet."

"We can use Dad's car. It's boring, but it's got wheels," Lori said.

"Why don't you call Uncle Joe? Maybe he'll let you drive his car if you're not going to be gone long."

"Yeah," Zack said. "Why didn't I think of that! His car is much cooler than yours. He's got a Beemer." The four of them ran back up the stairs as fast as they had run down.

Rock grinned as Will started laughing. "I guess I got my comeuppance," he said. "Wait until I tell Liz that Uncle Joe's car is way cooler than hers."

"It's a hazard of the preaching occupation," Will said. "If you wanted to drive a cooler car, you should have gone to medical school."

"Hey, I'm not complaining. I'm perfectly happy with my truck." He rinsed the fish off one last time and put them in freezer bags. "Here, I'll take the fish upstairs and put them in our refrigerator if you'll get rid of the fish guts and bones," he said.

"Thanks, why do I always get the ugly work? What should I do with them?"

"Put them in someone else's trash can," he said. Will laughed. "I'm kidding," Rock said. "Wrap them in the bag the ice came in and put them in our trash can - it has a liner in it. Garbage pickup is tomorrow anyway. The smell won't be so bad just for one night."

***

"I can't believe you just turned your keys over to them," John said to Joe after dinner.

"Zach assured me he's a good driver, John. Do I have any reason not to believe him?"

"Oh no, it's just an expensive car."

"I have insurance just like everybody else," he said. "And besides, it's nice to be the hero for once." He grinned at Rock. "I've always been in competition with Rock here, for my niece and nephew's attention. Now that I have something they like to drive, they won't give him the time of day."

"Well, let's see you get out on the beach with them and play volleyball," Rock said.

"I'll leave that up to you," Joe said. "Besides, you need to stay in shape. It looks like you'll be playing volleyball for about eighteen more years. Let's see, you'll be in your sixties, about the age I am now. Do you think you can keep up?"

"If not, I'll make Lori and Zack do it. It'll be payback time."

"I feel like I swallowed a volleyball," Liz said, "and it's playing a game of its own inside my stomach." Everyone looked down as she placed her hand on her tummy. "See!" The baby was active. "It looks like he's kicking and screaming, 'Let me out'!"

Joe walked over and put his hand on her stomach. "I hope you don't mind." He arched his eyebrows and looked down at Liz questioningly.

She laughed. "Well, I don't usually let men feel my stomach," she said. "But I'll make an exception for you, since you're the doctor."

He kept his hand in the same spot while the baby kicked. "How many weeks are you now?"

"Thirty-six," she answered. "June 27th is my due date."

"Any chance it could be earlier?" he asked.

"I don't think so," she answered. "Give or take a week or two. We got married on September 7th."

"Why do you ask?" Rock said.

"It looks like the baby has shifted position and dropped down into the pelvic area since we've been here. I make my living noticing things like that, you know." He grinned at Rock. "That doesn't usually happen until a little later in the pregnancy - usually around the thirty-seventh or thirty-eighth week."

"Do we need to be concerned?" Rock asked.

"No, no. I didn't mean to alarm you. You'll be back home next week anyway." He took his hand away. "I'll bring my stethoscope over tomorrow. And if this little fellow decides to make an early appearance, you've got the best ob/gyn doctor in Atlanta here with you." He winked at Liz.

"Modesty becomes you." Liz said, and winked back.

Joe walked back to the sofa where his friend Kathy was still seated. She was laughing at the exchange that had taken place between Joe and Liz. "Modesty is his middle name," she said. "But in all fairness, he does have the reputation of being one of the best."

"I paid her to say that," Joe said. He sat down and squeezed her hand. It was the first display of affection Liz had seen between the two, but the way they looked at each other now, she realized that it was more than just friendship they shared.

A car door shut in the garage below, and soon footsteps were rapidly ascending the stairs, sounding as Irene put it, like a herd of elephants. "Where's the fire?"

she asked, as the the four teens came rushing through the door.

"That's just it," Lori said. "It's out in the marsh again."

"What's out in the marsh again?" Will asked.

"A bonfire. Come look, Uncle Rock."

The men all got up and walked out on the second floor deck. Sure enough, a fire burned brightly in the same spot as it had before. Looking through Zach's binoculars, Rock could see shadows crossing between his line of vision and the fire. "I think it's time to go have a little discussion with the island police department," he said. "I'll drive up there tomorrow morning."

They stayed out on the deck and talked, watching the bonfire and discussing who it could be. Fires didn't just start themselves out in the middle of the marsh.

Zach interrupted and walked over to Joe. "I almost forgot, Uncle Joe," he said. He handed Joe his car keys. "Thanks for letting us borrow your car. Everybody was digging our ride," he said. "Can we borrow it again one night?"

"Sure, why not," Joe said.

"Yes!" Chloe said loudly, pumping her fist in the air. "But let me and Lori take a turn at riding in the front seat with you, Zack. You two guys hogged it all to yourselves tonight."

The sound of the elephant footsteps sounded again as all four of them scrambled up the stairs to the deck above. While the men were talking below, the kids were quietly plotting their plans for the next morning. Somehow, someway, they were going to find where the bonfire was coming from.

CHAPTER 19

"*A*nd the great dragon was thrown down, that ancient serpent, who is called the devil and Satan, the deceiver of the whole world—he was thrown down to the earth, and his angels were thrown down with him.*"*

- Revelation 12:9 ESV

Peterson's plans to take the canoe out changed when he saw how choppy the Intracoastal Waterway became after the storm. Instead, he drove his Jeep to the West End Resort and parked right inside the gate where the gatehouse still stood empty. Another car was parked right behind the gatehouse. It must belong to someone else walking on the beach. He locked the door and walked the beach to the entrance of the pathway, stooped down and walked in, quickly disappearing from sight. He marveled again at the consistent pattern of the imprints that made such a clear pathway through the undergrowth. Each one was smooth and as hard as concrete.

Something seemed different though, since the last time he'd been here with the old man. Some of the thick undergrowth seemed to have been cut back to make it easier to stand a little straighter rather than being in such a stooped position while navigating the path. He could actually see bits of what little light was still available in the sky as the sun rapidly began to set, whereas before, the scrubby brush and trees had formed an impenetrable canopy. He wondered if the old man, tall as he was, had started coming down here. Had to be - he was the only other person who knew the footpath's location. A faint glow from the pink sunset remained, but it wasn't enough to see where the steps were taking him. He pulled his flashlight out and turned it on. A few steps ahead, the light reflected on something shiny. Aha, the old man must have been coming here with his bottle. He had probably spent the entire fifty dollars he gave him on booze. He stepped closer and saw it was just a shiny Milky Way candy bar wrapper - more than likely blown in by the wind. It had been a while since he had been in from the beachside - maybe he had just thought the canopy was tighter. But no, here were some bare spots where branches had been broken off. An animal? He had seen deer tracks on the dunes earlier. Sure, that was it. He felt a little better, but he still shivered.

This was too spooky - it would be the last trip he made coming in from the beachside. When he came by boat, it was a straight shot, nothing hindering his progress except the marsh grass and a few sidewinder crabs. But tonight, something about the place filled him with a sense of dread. If I had any sense, I'd get out of here, he thought, but he kept going. He was almost to the center now. He would just put the fire log down, light it and hurry back down the same path. He would be home watching TV in thirty minutes.

The path ended and he was in the small clearing. Something wasn't quite right. Someone had been here. He looked around nervously. In the spot where he had built his previous fires, there was a small, flat table made of wood and a pile of brush ready to light.

"I'm getting out of here," he said aloud, just to hear his own voice and hoping to dispel the odd feeling that had come over him. He turned and headed for the path again, but just then a loud noise filled the air. Why, it sounded like a chicken squawking! He turned around and immediately wished he hadn't. The smell of lighter fluid and a quick swish of a match brought the pile of brush to life, flames licking up into the air. Not ten feet away from him loomed three dark figures. He couldn't see their features because of the backdrop glow of the fire, but they were all dressed in black.

"Stop right there!" one of them yelled, but it never entered his mind to stop. He went crashing through the brush and ran as fast as he could in his stooped over position, but it wasn't fast enough. He felt something tackle his ankles and take his feet straight out from under him. He went down head first on the cement-like imprint on the pathway. The last thing he saw was the flash of the Milky Way candy wrapper as it brushed against his eyelid.

***

A strong smell of blood assaulted his senses when he came to. He knew it must be his own from the feeling of dampness above his right eye. He tried to reach his hand up to his head, but realized that his hands were tied behind his back. He was in an upright position leaning against something prickly. If felt as if dozens of needles were sticking in his back. He could tell by the aromatic leaves he was crushing as he leaned against it, that it was a Hercules Club, one of the thorny scrub trees that covered the area. He'd had encounters with them before and they weren't pleasant. But the tree was the least of his worries.

The three dark figures were sitting in a semicircle around the fire. He didn't dare make a move for fear they would see he had regained consciousness. At first it seemed the men were talking low, but he then realized they were chanting something over and over. He looked around and his eyes settled on a small cage just a foot away. It looked like a cat carrier, but when his eyes adjusted to the light, he could see it was a live chicken. The chicken's eyes looked as terrified as he knew his must look. What were they going to do with a chicken? Could they be planning to eat it for dinner over the campfire? Poor bird! And then it hit him. What were they planning to do with him? Whatever it was, he knew he was in serious trouble. He hadn't prayed in a long time, but he still remembered how to do it. But would God listen to his prayer for help, when he himself was guilty of trying to deceive people for his own greedy gain? He bowed his head - he had nothing to lose.

***

"Must of cracked his head pretty hard, he's still out." It was the voice of one of the figures from the fire. Well, at least one part of his prayer had worked. With his head bowed, it must have appeared to the speaker that he was still unconscious.

Another voice answered from the direction of the fire. "Don't worry about him right now. Bring the hen over here." It was a woman's voice!

He heard the sound of the cage being picked up and the chicken started in on its squawking again, which grew louder as they lifted the bird out. "You know what to do." the woman said. She didn't sound very old - maybe in her early twenties. Suddenly the sound of a hatchet hitting wood filled the air and he couldn't help but be startled as the body of the headless chicken started flailing around on the ground.

Thank God, they hadn't seen him - they were so busy with the chicken. Both men caught it up and as he watched, the youngest one held it upside down above the fire as the woman held a large glass under its neck. He didn't have to pretend this time. He passed out cold.

***

He woke up with a splitting headache. It took his eyes a while to adjust to the dark, but when they did, they rested on the remnants of the fire. There were still a few glowing embers and he wondered how long his abductors had been gone. Were they coming back for him? He scrambled around trying to loosen his wrists from the tight ropes, but it was no use. They were so tight he had lost all feeling in them. He did manage to tumble his body forward and get away from the prickly bushes that had been his bed. When he did, he rolled over something on the ground beside him. It was a bottle of water and he wondered how it got there. With his hands tied, it would do him no good, though, and he was greedy with thirst. He was surprised they hadn't gagged him. He waited for a while until he was satisfied they were no longer around, and tried to scream, but very little sound came out. The combination of stress, inhaling smoke from the fire, and his excessive thirst caused his voice to be so hoarse, it was barely above a croak. The bottle of water became an obsession, like a mirage in the desert, and he tried fruitlessly to think of a way to open it and drink it.

He finally shifted enough so that his body could relax and drifted off to sleep. He dreamed that the cool liquid in the bottle was coursing down his lips and when he woke up next, it was to a gentle rain and a grey sky indicating it would soon be daylight. He opened his mouth wide trying to soak in every drop of rain he could. He knew he would need it as the day grew warm. He tried his voice again and was relieved that it was weak but audible. It was too early to try to scream for someone's attention, so he spent his time planning on how to make himself heard when the few tourists finally made their way down the beach. His best hope was the young group of kids that were staying on Pelican Pointe. He hoped they had seen the blazing fire during the night and would be curious enough to check out the dunes and beyond where he now lay. The rain chilled him and he scooted closer to the embers left from the fire. They were slowly sputtering out, but just as he got close enough, the rain suddenly stopped and within thirty minutes, the hints of pink in the sky told him that it would be a warm day.

As he checked out his surroundings, he noticed a large circle drawn in the sand, and inside the circle was a crude wooden cross, but it was stuck in the ground upside down. Seeing the cross turned that way seemed somehow sacrilegious. He hadn't gone to church in years, but even he knew the cross was a symbol that should be respected. "This is not good," he said aloud, and he renewed his effort to scream. This time he was successful, and shocked himself that he had screamed so loud. He kept it up for a minute or two until his voice started getting hoarse again, and gave it a rest.

He worked at getting his wrists free, and after about ten minutes of pulling and jerking on the cord, he was surprised when it broke free. He examined the cord when he pulled his hands from behind his back. It had a clean cut on one edge and then the ravels from where he had worked the rest of it loose. It looked as if someone had purposefully wanted him to get free. Were they planning to ambush him when he made his getaway?

The feet weren't so easy. The cord was tied so tight, there was very little blood circulating to his feet and they felt numb. He worked at the knots and wished that his fingernails were longer so he could get a good grip to work them out. After several minutes, he gave up and decided to try to scoot across the clearing and work his way down the crooked path using his arms to provide leverage. If he could just get out on the dunes where someone could see him.

It was working! His hands were getting torn up from the prickly bushes and the sharp stumps that had been cut, but he was so intent on getting out, he didn't feel it. About halfway down the path, he stopped to rest, and started screaming loudly once more. He couldn't believe it when he heard someone screaming back. Then it dawned on him that it could be the three people who had captured him last night, and was quiet a moment.

"Who is it and where are you?" He heard the voice and was relieved. His kidnappers knew who and where he was.

"Please help me. I'm back here in the brush," he shouted, and then started scooting on his backside once more.

The kids were standing on the highest dunes, but couldn't see anyone. "It's coming from the thicket over there," Chloe said, and pointed in the direction of the voice.

"Someone must have got stuck in there," Jake said. "And from the sound of it, he needs help."

Zack started searching for a way in. "Maybe it's the person who built the fire last night, but how are we going to find him. He sounds like he's in trouble, alright." He turned to Lori. "Run back and get Uncle Rock. I have a feeling we're going to need him."

"Come on, Chloe," Lori said as she took off. Both girls were on the cross country team at school, and they ran as fast as their feet would carry them."

***

"Did the motion camera pick up any chicken snatchers last night?"

Charlie was adjusting the camera on the fence for a better angle. Rock had walked down the back steps to take the food scraps from their breakfast to the outside trash bin. They had learned early on that even a crumb left on the table would attract more ants than Rock had seen collectively throughout his entire lifetime.

"Nope! No chicken thievin' going on last night. The only action I saw was a couple of lovebirds walking hand in hand past the chicken coop on the way to your house."

"Can't imagine who that could have been," Rock said with mock surprise.

"Me either," Charlie said. He looked at Rock and grinned, "I was a little disappointed that it was PG rated."

They both turned around as Chloe and Lori arrived, galloping like horses across the boardwalk and down the steps, and calling Rock's name.

"Uncle Rock, come quick!" Lori got to him first, but Chloe was right on her heels. "And hurry, someone's in trouble on the beach."

Rock took one look at them and realized that they were serious. He turned to Charlie. "Would you go up and tell Liz where I've gone. She'll be worried if I don't come back right away." He put the plate down on the steps. "Lead the way, girls," he said, and they all three took off running.

They got back to the boys just as Zack spotted Peterson making his way out of the undergrowth that led to the path. Zack waved with both arms, "This way!" By the time Rock reached them, Zack was bending down over the strange little man trying to make sense of what he was saying.

Zack turned to Rock. "He's so upset, I can't understand a thing he's saying. Sounds like gibberish to me."

"Let's get these ropes off his feet," Rock said, and pulled his utility knife out of his pocket. "This is supposed to cut seat belts," he said. "Let's see how it works on this heavy rope." The razor sharp feature of the knife cut right through the ropes, and he kneeled before the man and started massaging his ankles and feet. "The rope was tight," he said. "Do you have any feeling in your feet?

The man had calmed down when he saw that an adult was taking charge. "They're numb," he said, "but that's helping."

Rock continued to rub the man's ankles while checking him over. "You've got a lot of cuts and scratches," he said. "And that looks like dried blood on the back of your head."

"This is our Uncle Rock," Zack said. "He's a preacher."

The man looked into the eyes of his rescuer and then down at the ground. "A preacher," he said. "That's good.., because I need to confess my sins."

Rock pulled his phone out. "I'm going to call the police. This looks serious."

"Yeah," Peterson said. "We should call the police." He struggled to get up, but he had been in the same position so long, his leg muscles wouldn't cooperate."

"Maybe we should call an ambulance," Chloe said.

"No, no, I'll be okay as soon as I get my legs moving."

Rock looked through his contacts until he found *Beach Police*. He had looked up the number when he and Liz got back to the cottage last night and entered it in his phone. He had planned on calling today anyway to report the fire burning in the marsh. As it was ringing, John, Will and Robert walked up.

"What's all the commotion," Will asked, then looked down and saw the man lying on the sand. Liz had gone to tell the others what Charlie had told her, so Will had picked up the first aid box and a towel before coming down the beach. He handed the towel to Jake. "Run get this wet in the surf. This man needs to be cleaned up. That's a nasty head wound. Did you call in for a rescue?"

"A police officer is on the way," he said, putting his phone back in his pocket. "He can call rescue if he needs more attention." He paused. "I hear a siren now."

Peterson became agitated and called to Rock, "Preacher, do you mind if I talk to you before the police get here?"

Rock knelt down. "It'll take them a few minutes to walk down to the beach after they park. What can I do for you?"

"Pray," he said. "They'll be after me now for sure. I'd rather be in a room full of snakes than those evil bastar~. Uh oh, I'm sorry, I didn't mean to cuss..., it's just that...."

Rock cut him off. "Who are they? And how did you get in there - there's nothing but thick undergrowth."

"There's just a few feet of brush, then it's the Devil's Footpath." He pointed in the direction of the path. "And it's rightly named since it was devil worshipers who did this." He looked down. "But I was somewhere I shouldn't have been. If I hadn't been so greedy, none of this would've happened." He looked back up at Rock. "Does God forgive people for being deceitful and greedy...and trying to cheat people?"

Rock nodded. "He will if you believe in Him and are sincerely repentant," he said.

Peterson looked sheepish. "I do, but somewhere along the way I got caught up in other things. And I guess if I feel awful about what I've been doing, I'm repentant, right?"

Rock nodded his head. "I'll pray, but you'll need to do your part too. It's a simple prayer and He listens, I promise." The man repeated the prayer that Rock had prayed.

"How do I know if He forgave me?" he said.

"He knows when you're sincere. Here, I've got a pen and a card in my pocket. Write down your name and phone number and I'll follow up with you and help you find a good church and mentor down here when I get back home. Look, here's the police officer already." He looked up and read the officer's nameplate, Detective Wilson Garrett, Island Beach Police Dept. "Detective Garrett," he said. "I'm glad you're here."

Will had been working on the man's wounds while Rock had been talking to him, and after cleaning the dried blood out of his hair, it was apparent that he needed medical attention. He mentioned it to the officer and he agreed.

"Sir, we'll get your report when you get to the hospital." He put Will's towel under the man's head and lowered him to the ground. "I took the liberty of calling Rescue before I left the station, just in case. They should be here in about..," he looked at his watch, "two minutes." The sound of sirens filled the air and everyone looked up at the detective. "A slow day for emergencies...," he said, and shrugged his shoulders.

Tess and Ove were standing amidst the tall sea oats about a hundred yards away, near the steps leading to the West End Resort. They watched for a moment, then hurried to their car. She started the engine and drove quickly away while all the attention was on the beach.

"How did he get away?" Tess asked. She looked accusingly at Ove.

"I don't know. He was tied tight enough. I watched the kid with the rope. He's a good one with knots. His old man was a shrimper. He's dead now, but the kid's been around boats long enough to know how to tie a good knot." He watched as she slammed her hand on the steering wheel. She was biting her lip hard enough to bring blood. He had seen her this way before and it wasn't good. He tried to think of something to calm her down. "I think it was too dark for him to see us clearly. He couldn't possibly identify us."

"It's your job to see that he doesn't. They'll be taking him to the hospital. He's probably got a concussion from the fall he took. There was a lot of blood." She paused for a moment. "And why did he get so cozy with the man who was kneeling beside him. Probably praying... or telling him about us. I'll take care of that." A strange sound came from her lips, and Ove looked at her again. It was a laugh, he realized, an odd laugh, bordering on hysteria. An evil laugh, but what did he expect, a sweet angelic laugh?

Hell no, this was Tess, so beautiful and seductive when he first met her. He would have done anything for her - still would, he guessed. What had he got himself into? He was no saint - he'd had his share of trouble, but this was different, and all of a sudden, he was scared.

CHAPTER 20

"*Be strong in the Lord and in his mighty power. Put on the full armor of God so that you can take your stand against the devil's schemes. For our struggle is not against flesh and blood, but against the rulers, against the authorities, against the powers of this dark world and against the spiritual forces of evil in the heavenly realms.*"

- Ephesians 6:10-11 NIV

Ove

He was in luck. It was the lunch hour and there was a replacement receptionist, a local girl who had been in some of his high school classes. He looked at her nametag - Mandy Robbins.

"Hey Mandy. I haven't seen you in a while. I'm looking for a patient brought in by ambulance this morning. He dropped his cell phone on the beach when they picked him up. I figured he might need it." He waved his own cell phone in front of her.

"Oh, yeah," she said. "I couldn't live without my phone." She looked at the patient list. "He's the only person who's been admitted today. Room 414 - you'll have to go around to the front to get in though. I don't have the code to let you in back here." She paused, "Or you can wait about five minutes for Mildred to get back. She has the code."

"I'll go around front," he said. "I'm in a hurry and Mildred may be late getting back."

"Not Mildred," she said, but he was already out the door. He knew Mildred. He had dated her daughter once, and Mildred didn't like him.

The elevator doors were just opening when he came around the corner. A nurse had just got on, so he walked in behind her and the door closed. She pushed the button and turned around and asked him which floor he needed. "Four," he replied, without looking up. He noticed that she looked uncomfortable to be on the elevator alone with him and she stood as near the door as possible. He could have kicked himself for not taking the stairs. At the second floor, a white-haired lady, who looked a lot like his grandmother got on. It reminded him that he hadn't seen his Grandma in over a year, ever since she had tried to discourage him from getting any more tattoos, and he had stormed out her door. Another reason he should have taken the stairs.

The door closed and the nurse asked her which floor she needed. "First floor," she said with a smile.

"Ma'am, this elevator is going up. I'm afraid you got on the wrong one."

"Oh, honey, I didn't get on the wrong elevator," she said. "It just means I have to go up to get back down." She laughed as if it made perfect sense. The nurse smiled and nodded, but he didn't even acknowledge her. "The Lord never makes a mistake and He told me to get on this elevator." She paused. "Well, He put me in front of it anyway, and that's just as good as telling me to get on."

She smiled sweetly. "What else are you going to do when a door opens up in front of you?"

She had some small pamphlets in her hand and gave one to the nurse, and then turned around and looked at him. He was surprised that she didn't look at all his tattoos with revulsion. She didn't show any fear or hesitation - she just held a pamphlet out to him as if he was a clean cut all-American college student. "Here's one for you too, young man." He took it and crammed it in his pocket to keep from making a scene.

He saw the number four flash above the elevator and couldn't wait to get off once the door opened. The nurse was going up to the fifth floor, so she stood aside for him step out. He made a move to get off, but stopped short when he saw two police officers standing at the nurse's station ahead. One of them was the officer from the beach. "Damn," he said under his breath, and then aloud, he said," Uh, this isn't my floor - I forgot, my uncle is on the third floor," and stepped back in as far as he could get in the corner.

The nurse gave him a suspicious look, and the white-haired lady made her way to the door. "Oh, then, it must be where I'm supposed to get off. I never know where the Lord will lead me. Like I said, he doesn't make mistakes." She saw the room number where the police officers stood. "Ah, Room 414 - this must be the place I'm supposed to be. I dreamed about the number 414 last night. I'll see if these nice men will let me go in."

The nurse hesitated, but pushed the close door button when she realized he wasn't going to get off. At the fifth floor, he got off behind her and made his way to the stairwell. "I think I'll just take the stairs back down," he mumbled.

The nurse walked over to the nurse's station, looking over her shoulder the whole time to see if he was really going to the stairwell.

"Oops," said a voice right in front of her. "You were about to run me over, Susan." She looked up and found she had almost collided with her supervisor. "Are you okay?"

"Just a little spooked. That was one strange looking dude on the elevator with me."

"Do you think we need to call security?" her supervisor asked.

"No, he seemed harmless enough, just strange...the tattoos, I guess."

Ove ran down the five flights of steps, then walked slowly as not to call attention to himself, going out the front door and then to his car. He was glad to see there were no police officers in the parking lot. He got in his car and looked around, trying to figure out what to do now. It had been a couple of years since he had been to Southport so he decided to go down to the waterfront and sit for awhile. No one would look for him there.

He parked on a side street about a block away and walked the rest of the way. It was 1:30 and the lunch traffic had cleared out, so he had his choice of what bench he wanted. He took one facing the water and watched as two fishing boats came in from the Cape Fear. He couldn't remember when he had felt this peaceful. The weed he smoked often put him in a trance-like state, but it wasn't peace. Somehow, today, he had a clarity of mind that he hadn't had lately, and with it came the knowledge and determination that he was going to stay away from Tess. The animals and chickens last summer hadn't bothered him so much, except for the dog.

Last summer had gone by in a blur. Tess had stayed stoned half the time, and she seemed to have a never ending supply of the stuff, giving him all he wanted. When she disappeared during the winter, he stopped doing drugs and his head was clearer, but now that she was back he'd started dabbling in it again. He didn't understand all this chanting stuff and what she called sacrificing animals. Chickens were one thing, but this talk of getting rid of people, he didn't want any part of it. But where could he go that she wouldn't find him?

He got fidgety and felt around in his pocket. He needed a joint - he knew he had rolled one this morning, but where was it? He felt a piece of paper in his pocket thinking it was a packet of cigarette paper wrappers, but it was the folded up pamphlet the old lady had given him. He cursed and almost threw it on the ground, but then thought better of it. They were cracking down on littering - signs were everywhere along with plenty of trash receptacles. He certainly didn't need to take any chances today.

He opened up the pamphlet. It was one of those blasted Bible tracts like the people in his Granny's church were always pushing on people. "I wish those Bible thumpers would mind their own business," he said out loud, and started to fold it up again, but he saw a scrawled, wavy handwriting across the bottom. "You were in my path today and God doesn't make mistakes."

"What the Hell?" he said. He read a few lines of the tract and folded it back up. With tears in his eyes he knew what he would do. It was time to pay a visit to Granny.

The forty-five minute ride was worth it. When his grandmother opened the door and saw him standing there, she opened her arms. Her big heart more than made up for her short stature and he reached down and put both his arms around her. Her familiar scent of lavender soap brought back childhood memories of crawling into her lap to hear one of her many stories. How had he drifted so far away from Granny, the person who loved him more than anyone in the world?

He remembered distinctly the verses she read to him every time his mother would pick him up for her weekend visits, knowing he would be around the lowlife boyfriends she always seemed to pick up. First they were simple verses, "*So do not fear, for I am with you.*" Then during his teen years when he was so easily influenced, she dug a little deeper.

"*Finally, be strong in the Lord and in his mighty power. Put on the full armour of God so that you can take your stand against the devil's schemes,*' she had read. "Just imagine a knight in King Arthur's court, Johnny," she had said, "putting on his armor to go out and fight. First his breastplate, then his helmet, and finally his sword and shield."

King Arthur's court, ha! That story was for kids, wasn't it? But now he just wished he'd had the sense to listen.

Tess

Where was he? They had arranged to meet at his trailer at 8 o'clock for an update on what he had done about Peterson. She knew he didn't have the heart and wouldn't have the opportunity to get rid of Peterson. The police would be crawling all over the place. Now, she on the other hand...., her desire for killing things was getting stronger. It had been in the back of her mind all winter what it would be like to take a human life. At first it was frightening, but the longer she thought about it, it became almost like an obsession. She had been tempted when they had captured Peterson, but Ove had talked her out of it. Now look where it had got them. It would have been so easy. Now sketches of their faces would likely be all over the newspapers if the man could identify them. Of course, it would have been difficult for him to see them in the darkness. Maybe he was no threat after all.

Kidnapping was a federal offense, a serving time in prison offense. Murder was worse - prison for life or a possible death penalty. She didn't have any desire to go to prison again, although the time she'd spent there for shoplifting had been when she'd found her purpose and she had joined a satanic cult when she had been released. After she had drifted down from Maryland to the North Carolina coast, she hadn't found any local chapters to join, so she had started her own with the ragtag twosome she now had.

One was just a kid. Geir hated his stepfather and was furious with his mother, so he had latched on when she met him one day and gave him an ounce of attention. He was moldable with no one to really care if he came home late at night.

Ove now, he had potential. She had reeled him in, just as she had been trained to do to get new converts to Satan. She started out by being sweet and attentive, made him fall head over heels in love with her, then slowly gained control over him. She had him right under her thumb. He needed her and she needed him. He was her voice of reason and had so far kept her from getting into trouble. She would use him, but didn't think he would take too kindly when she started doing the same with new converts. Her sexuality was her biggest strength, her mentor had told her, and she should use it.

She needed new recruits and had set out to bring some of Ove's buddies into the cult, but she hadn't counted on his jealousy, so they were still stuck at the three of them for now. She would have to go out on her own - maybe to some of the sleazier bars in Wilmington. She had made a lot of money in those sleazy bars. She'd slip something in a guy's drink, then take him outside. When he passed out, she would pick his wallet and leave. They were usually too embarrassed to make a police report.

Her thoughts went back to revenge. Those kids had found the foot path. When the police arrived, she and Ove had left the beach. She dropped him off at his trailer, and then couldn't resist going back to the resort to watch from a safe distance. She'd seen the kids coming out of the entrance to the path, them and that boring, middle-aged guy - the one with the pregnant wife. She had seen the two of them earlier on the beach, all kissy-kissy - 'bout made her sick on her stomach. And he'd been the one Peterson had been confiding in. Her eyes lit up. Revenge - now she knew how to get it.

She looked at her cellphone for the third time. Midnight - the magic hour. Ove must have got himself thrown in jail. But he wouldn't tell them about her. She was confident that she had him totally under her spell. No one could save him now.

She cranked the car and pulled away from the trailer. She was unaware that Ove was wrapped up in a warm afghan asleep on his grandmother's sofa. She had never experienced the love and fervent prayers of a grandmother and had no idea those prayers could be far more powerful than her spells.

CHAPTER 21

"*L*ove is patient and kind; love does not envy or boast;
it is not arrogant."

- 1 Corinthians 13:4 ESV

"So there's not a ghost, after all?" They had finished dinner and were sitting in the large living room of the house Will and Irene had rented. With its large open living area and five bedrooms, it was the perfect size house for the two of them and their daughters' families.

"No, Mom," Rock said, "but if Mr. Peterson is right, it's a lot more sinister than that - an occult, possibly satanic. I'm sure there'll be a police presence here for the next few days until they finish their investigation."

"That's scary," she said. "It's a shame all this happened on our vacation."

"Don't worry - with the police around, we'll be safer than ever, although I was sure they would be here this afternoon with some questions for me and the kids, since we were the ones who spoke to him first."

Liz covered her mouth and tried to suppress a yawn, but Rock noticed. "I think I need to get this sleepyhead home and in bed," he said, and got up from his chair.

"Y'all sleep tight," Irene said. "It's been quite a day - I know you must be worn out, Liz."

"I don't think I'll have any trouble sleeping tonight," she said. "Good night, everyone."

As they walked by Charlie's chicken house, Rock stopped and pulled Liz into his arms. "Let's give Charlie something to talk about tomorrow when he looks at his security tape," and proceeded to give her a long, lingering kiss.

***

"Up and at 'em."

A feather-like kiss touched his cheek, and Rock opened his eyes to sunlight streaming through the shades on the bedroom windows.

"I slept late," Rock said, yawning and then stretching his arms over his head.

"No, I just got up early," Liz said. "Do you realize we've only got three more days of vacation left and I want to enjoy every minute of it. This week has flown by!"

She was already dressed and Rock thought she looked almost ethereal in a white linen long sleeved blouse against the backdrop of the sun-filled room. She looked sun-kissed, from the healthy glow of her cheeks, to the touch of tan on her long slender legs. "You look beautiful," he said. "I take it you've had your first cup of coffee or you wouldn't be quite so chipper and ready for the day to start."

"I have, and here's yours," she said, putting it down on the bedside table. "I have breakfast ready too. And the reason I'm so chipper is because I slept so well for a change. I didn't wake up a single time last night."

"I know," he said. "You were out like a light while I was watching the minutes, then hours tick away on the clock until about 2 a.m. I think I caught your insomnia."

"I'm sorry, you can go back to sleep if you want. I can keep the bacon warm - I haven't cooked the eggs yet."

"Oh, no - if my beautiful wife is going to be up, I'm going to be up." He sat on the side of the bed and picked up his coffee. "Just give me a few minutes to put on a tee shirt and brush my teeth."

She looked pleased and started back to the kitchen. "Scrambled or fried?" she asked.

"Surprise me."

"What do we have planned today?" he asked, as he spread jelly on his toast. "Hey, this is Mabel's jelly! How did you manage that?"

She grinned. "Mabel came by before we left home with three jars. She said it was all she had left until blackberry picking time in July."

"And she gave them to me!" Rock said, in awe.

"Us," Liz corrected, "and I only brought one with us." She spread a heaping tablespoon of it on her toast and took a bite.

"And why did you wait all week before opening it, may I ask? Rock arched his eyebrows and gave her a questioning look.

She laughed at his expression. "Because you would have polished it off in two days."

"You're right." He eyed the big glob she had spread on her toast, but conceded that he would sound petty if he told her the truth - that she was eating more than he was. He remembered his mother's words, "Never comment on how much a woman is eating if you want to keep your teeth in your head," she would say when he complained about his sisters eating all the snack food. He decided to change the subject. "You never said what you want to do today?"

"The rest of the family are riding down to Myrtle Beach this morning, so it will be just you and me again." She winked. "So, how about long walks on the beach this morning to pick up shells. I promised Reva I would bring her some back. Then lunch and maybe an afternoon nap. It's Joe's turn to fix dinner tonight - our turn is tomorrow night, so we should go shopping later for the ingredients for the chicken bog."

"Sounds like a good plan, especially the nap part. I'll get dressed. Just so we don't have a repeat of yesterday's excitement."

"Do you think they've caught the people responsible for tying up that poor man?

"I don't know. Detective Garrett said he would call us when they do, but I have a feeling they are long gone from here. They wouldn't want to chance being recognized, although Mr. Peterson said he wouldn't be able to pick them out of a line-up. He was unconscious, or pretending to be most of the time. He said he would never forget the woman's voice though."

"You think it's the people you saw with the tattoos," don't you?"

"I do, and I think they're dangerous. The detectives were supposed to come out late yesterday to do a thorough search of the area, but I didn't see them, did you? Someone had built an altar and had apparently been stealing Charlie's chickens to do a live sacrifice. Like Mr. Peterson said, it could be a satanic cult. One of the dead giveaways was the upside down cross."

Liz shuddered. "A blatant mockery of Jesus," she said.

"We learned a lot about cults in seminary," he said, "but to be honest, I haven't given it much thought since it doesn't seem to be a problem in Park Place. I need to take a refresher course when we get back home. We ministers need to be aware of signs and symbols of that sort of thing. We like to hide our heads in the sand and pretend it doesn't exist, but it does."

The morning was cool and windy, so the walk on the beach wasn't a good idea. With sand blowing in their faces, they gave up and went back inside.

"Well, that wasn't very pleasant, was it?" Liz said. "Why don't we go into town to get what we need, then we'll hit the beach after lunch. Maybe the wind will be calm by then."

"If not, there's always the afternoon nap to look forward to," Rock said, with a twinkle in his eye.

"You insatiable beast," she said. She tried to swat him with a magazine she picked up from the counter, but he ducked. Laughing, she tried again. This time he let her, but pulled her close to him when the magazine made contact.

"Hmm," he said, looking down at her face. "It's your fault for being so irresistible, especially with that little scattering of freckles across your nose."

She groaned. "And I used sunscreen. I should have known I would get more freckles."

"I love them," he said. "My grandmother always called them sun kisses when my sisters would come in out of the sun complaining about their freckles."

"That sounds better than freckles," she said. "Maybe I should just embrace my sun kisses instead of wishing them away."

He reached down and kissed her nose. "We had better get a move on if we want to shop, walk on the beach and take a nap before dinner tonight."

The wind was much calmer when they came back. They put their groceries away and went back out on the beach after lunch. They walked east toward the pier, then back again, finding a few shells along the way. They sat on the beach for a while, but had to move their chairs when the high tide came in. "You can tell it's a full moon," Rock said. "The tide is always higher on a full moon. Let's go back in. I feel a nap coming on."

"Yes, and I'm thirsty. We forgot to bring our thermos of iced tea when we came down."

Rock was sound asleep when she came back from the kitchen. She smiled at the sight of him. "So much for irresistible!" she said out loud. She lay down beside him, but couldn't get comfortable. She got up and read for awhile and then decided to go back out on the beach. The tide was finally going out leaving lots of shells in its wake. She picked up her bag she used to collect shells and hurried *down* the stairs looking in both directions. There seemed to be considerably more shells washed up on the west end, so she headed that way. There were more small shells than big ones, but she stopped at each place the tide had dumped them and combed through each pile with her toes. The further she walked, the bigger the shells got, and before she knew it she had gone farther than she intended. Her bag wasn't quite full, but when she turned and looked in the direction she had come, she was surprised to see how far she had walked. She could see the windsock on the deck of Edie's house, but it seemed to be at least a quarter of a mile away. The two small dinghy sailboats that had been beached on the sand were just beyond the beach access steps leading up to the resort. She looked back in the direction she had been walking and realized that she was almost at the end of the island where the houses on the West End Winter Resort stopped. She had better start back. She hadn't left Rock a note and he would be worried when he woke up.

CHAPTER 22

"While it is said, Today if you will hear his voice, harden not your hearts, as in the provocation."

- Hebrews 3:15 KJV

Tess had finally reached Ove the next day after his visit to his grandmother's. She hadn't asked where he had been, and he hadn't volunteered, but they had arranged to meet on the back deck of the West End Clubhouse. She had suggested that they wear jeans and a plain white t-shirt so they would blend in with the other workers who had been in and out making repairs on the cottages just in case there were any cops still hanging about.

Ove was nervous. He wanted to tell Tess he had decided to make a clean break, but he didn't know how she would take it. He had seen her violent side and didn't like it. He knew he could physically handle her but the psyche effect she had on him was something else. It was as if something powerful and dark was acting as a magnet to pull him deep down into a place he didn't want to go. He hadn't confided in his grandmother the night before, but she had sensed something was wrong and had put both her hands on his shoulder and prayed over him as only a grandmother can do before he left her house.

He was pulled in two directions. He wanted to scoff at her religious ways, but found himself just standing there, letting her pray for him. He didn't want to admit it, but there was something comforting in her prayer that made him feel warm and safe. "Don't allow your heart to be hardened to God, Johnny," she had pleaded with him after her prayer, but he thought it may be a little too late for that.

He parked behind one of the cottages nearby and walked to the clubhouse. Tess's car was parked behind the clubhouse, but she wasn't in it. He opened the car door. Her keys were inside. He looked in the back seat but saw nothing but the overnight case she always left in the car in case she spent the night at his place. He had a feeling that his wasn't the only place she spent nights. She would be gone days at a time leaving no word about her whereabouts, something he had tried to ignore until now.

He walked up the stairs to the deck of the clubhouse and turned one of the handles of the big french doors. It was still locked, so she must have taken a walk. He tried to look inside the building, but the tinted glass on the patio doors created a mirror effect in the sun. He stepped up close to the glass and peered inside. The room covered a large expanse and had casual seating throughout. Two large sofas separated by a tall, narrow table were pushed against the wall facing the doorway. A lamp and a stack of brochures were on the table, a clock hung on the wall above the table. The clock hands showed ten past two, and he and Tess were supposed to meet at two. There were no chairs on the deck. He supposed they had all been put in storage when the residents had left to keep the summer storms from blowing them away. The whole place looked deserted, but he could hear hammering coming from a house a couple of blocks away. The temperature was in the mid-eighties - not so hot as to be uncomfortable, but just enough to make him drowsy, especially since he didn't get much sleep at Granny's house the night before. The overhang of the clubhouse provided a little shade, so he sat on the floor with his back against the siding and dozed off.

Tess had pulled into the gate at 1:45. She didn't see Ove's car anywhere so she drove around to see how many people were working in the resort. There was one work van at a house on the marsh side of the complex with two men on a ladder putting up gutters. They glanced as she drove by, but continued working when they didn't recognize her. She had a baseball cap pulled down over her eyes and with her thin frame, she could pass for a boy. She drove back down the main street, but still no sign of Ove. He was never in a rush to get anywhere. She parked out of sight behind the clubhouse and got out of the car. She wanted to stay out of sight, but was curious to see if there were any police officers still looking for leads. There had been one small article in The Beacon, but it had been consigned to the third page news after being usurped by news of a drug sting operation and a bank holdup in Shallotte.

She climbed the steps to the boardwalk leading to the beach and concealing herself behind a post, looked east toward the Devil's Footpath. All seemed to be quiet. She scanned the beach in the other direction and saw a lone figure walking. It was a woman and she was carrying a beach bag. And she was also very pregnant. Tess walked across the boardwalk and descended the steps to the beach. As she sat on the bottom step and waited, dark and obsessive thoughts took over any common sense she may have had. Things were looking up. This was the wife of the preacherman. Yes, they were looking up indeed.

As Liz made her way back up the beach, her eyes were on the sand trying to spot any sharks teeth or abalone shells she might have missed. She looked up again to see how much progress she had made. Her back cramped a little from all the stooping she had done. Now she was wishing she had waited for Rock to wake from his nap so he could have come with her. Not far ahead was the beach entry to the resort. It had just crossed her mind that she could stop for a while and rest on the steps when she saw someone ahead already sitting on them. The person had on a cap, but had his head turned her way as if he was staring at her. When he didn't move and just kept staring, she became uneasy. She looked around to see if there was any other way to get across the dunes. The dunes were high and the sand so soft, it would just crumble beneath her feet if she tried to climb. She decided to just keep walking. There was nowhere else to go. When she got a little closer, she looked up, intending to smile and not show any signs of fear. "Make eye contact," a self defense expert had once told her. But what she saw made the smile freeze before it started. Cold gray eyes stared at her out of a face covered in tattoos. The baseball cap came off and Liz saw it was a woman, and knew without a doubt it was the suspect who had tied up the man in the marsh. She started running, but the girl darted out in front of her. She knew it was no use and started saying the twenty-third Psalm aloud. "The

Lord is my shepherd; I shall not want. He maketh me to lie down in green pastures, He leadeth me...."

The young woman grabbed her arm and twisted it behind her. "Shut up and walk slowly up those steps."

Liz did as she was told. If she pushed her down, it would hurt the baby. She felt calmer now, and quietly, under her breath continued the Psalm, "Yea, though I walk through the valley of the shadow of death, I will fear no evil: for thou art with me; thy rod and thy staff they comfort me." She felt a push from behind and fell hard to her knees.

CHAPTER 23

"*B*ut the Lord is faithful, He will strengthen and protect you from the evil one."

- 2 Thessalonians 3:3 NASV

Ove had only dozed for a few minutes when he heard footsteps running up the steps of the deck. He looked up expecting to see Tess, but it was the kid, the one she called Geir, who had been hanging around them for a while. He didn't know why Tess encouraged this kid - he couldn't be over 16. "Pull 'em in while they're young and impressionable," Tess had said. "The kid's old man died a few years back and he hates his stepfather because now his mother's pregnant. He's a rotten little brat, but that's the kind we need. With all that hate pent up inside, he's an easy convert."

But when Geir stopped in front of him, he didn't look like he was filled with hate. He looked like a frightened kid. Maybe he should talk to him and tell him to get out while he could. He got up from where he had been sitting. The kid was stuttering, trying to get his words out.

"What is it?" he asked, then looked around, wondering if the cops were close by. "How did you get here?"

"I rode my bike. It-it-it's Tess," he stuttered. "She chased a pregnant woman down on the beach and she's coming this way. The woman fell down but she twisted her arm and made her get up."

Ove rolled his eyes. "What has she done now?" He walked to the edge of the deck and looked up the street. He saw Tess coming with the woman slightly in front of her. It almost looked like they were just going for a stroll. "Kid, you'd be better off if you left now. Just get on your bike and ride home." Geir just stood there with his mouth open, as if frozen to the spot.

***

After her scripture recitation, Liz felt strangely calm - not that she wasn't scared - she was frightened out of her wits, but she just had a feeling that no matter what happened, God was there with her and her unborn child. She had been pushed from behind and fallen on her knees, but she had been able to get up and keep walking. She saw two young men on the steps of the clubhouse up ahead and hoped they would help her, but they just stepped aside.

***

When Tess had forced her up the stairs, she had taken a small instrument and jiggled it inside the door lock. It took only a few seconds and the knob turned easily. When they were all inside, she shut the door and pulled a large vertical blind across the opening of what looked to be a large gathering room. Still twisting Liz's arm, she half pushed, half carried her to a back room where it was much darker. It looked to be a small dining hall where refreshments for social gatherings were served. Commercial style dining chairs were stacked against a wall and several small round tables were placed throughout the room. A large china cabinet was against the back wall where Tess had forced her to sit on the floor.

She took a look at the room inside the building where Tess had forcibly pushed and shoved her. The young boy in the room was quiet and seemed to be much gentler than the one called Tess had been. "Tie her up!" Tess had commanded. "And gag her so she can't call out."

Liz had looked pleadingly in his eyes. "Please...I'm pregnant. If you're going to tie my hands, please tie them in front so it won't be such a strain. I'm begging you not to hurt my baby."

He blushed and looked down at his feet. "Just do what I say ma'am and you won't get hurt." Was he trying to sound much tougher than he was? It was hard to gauge what he was thinking without being able to look in his eyes. Why he's just a boy, she thought, when he finally looked up. Even the tattoo on his neck wasn't real - it was henna, she now realized as she looked at him more closely. She had learned to recognize when a tattoo was real or not while working so closely with high school students in her counseling job. And the look he gave her - almost like he was ashamed of what he was doing. Maybe there was some hope after all, but her hopes were dashed when he tied her hands, he tied them tight, but at least tied them in front as she had asked. She was thankful for small things.

"Does that hurt?" he asked. She nodded and he loosened them slightly so as not to cut off circulation. He looked around the room for something to gag her with. He opened the china cabinet and pulled out two linen table napkins. He worked with one, folding it this way and that, then finally folded it into a triangle. His talk was tough again. "If you promise not to scream out, I'll just tie it around your mouth instead of stuffing it down your throat."

"How did you get mixed up in this?" she asked, trying to read his eyes.

"Shut up!" he said in a louder tone of voice. "This will shut you up," he said harshly, looking around to see if Tess was close by. He put the napkin snugly across her mouth and tied it tightly behind her ears. She was propped up with her back against a wall. He got out another length of rope and tied her feet together.

Tess and the other young man who had been waiting on the porch were in a heated discussion. Liz was having trouble making out what they were saying. There was no doubt that Tess's voice was the one dominating the conversation, but then he raised his voice. "You think we were in trouble before - just wait if anything happens to her!" He pointed to Liz. "I don't want any part of it! I'm through!"

A truly evil persona seemed to take over the girl's features. "You're through when I say you're through," she said. A cloud of darkness seemed to hang in the room and Liz shivered. The young man was taken aback, but after a few minutes regained his composure.

"Let her loose, Tess," he pleaded. "It will take her at least twenty minutes to walk back to her house and by that time, we'll be in our cars and out of the county. I know plenty of places to hide."

A loud and ungodly laughter filled the air and Tess' voice seemed an octave lower. "Are you crazy?" she shouted. "I have plans for her." She looked over at Liz. "And that baby she's carrying." Liz cringed and slid further down on the floor as Tess continued her rant. "Her husband is the reason we no longer have a place to worship - he and those kids." She let out a string of curse words and stomped her feet.

Liz was confused. What did Rock have to do with this woman's anger? She wasn't being reasonable. Witnessing the hate and fury in Tess's face, she finally realized she was dealing with someone who had snapped. She was tall and thin and Liz watched as she pushed the young man aside, and in trepidation, watched each step she took until she reached her side. She reached down and with both hands, grabbed Liz's hair and pulled her upwards. When Liz cried out, she let go of her hair and laughed as Liz fell hard back to a sitting position on the floor. She watched in horror as Tess stepped back and then pulled her foot back in a position to kick. She was stuck - she couldn't move out of the way. All she could think of was to utter the first scripture that came to mind, "*He will cover you with his feathers. He will shelter you with his wings. His faithful promises are your armor and your protection.*" She closed her eyes and waited for the blow. The last thing she remembered before she blacked out was the young man shouting, "Tess!" and the sound of feet running toward them. Then came the pain.

CHAPTER 24

"*To the pure all things are pure: but to them that are defiled and unbelieving nothing is pure; but both their mind and their conscience are defiled.*"

- Titus 1:15 NASV

Rock woke from his nap with a start, then looked at the alarm clock on the table. 2:35! Why had Liz let him sleep so long? It had been a good two hours since they'd had lunch. Liz had said she would tidy up the kitchen and join him for a nap in a few minutes, but he must have dozed off immediately. He admitted to himself that he felt refreshed after the nap. He was going to be in for a rude awakening when he got back into the real world and couldn't take naps. Walking into the kitchen, then the living room, he called out to Liz. When she didn't answer, he walked out on the deck and looked on the beach. The whole family was there and the kids were playing in the water. Relieved that she must have joined them, he walked down with his beach towel and chair.

The children saw him coming and came running, wrapping wet and sandy arms around him. He dropped his beach chair and picked Rachel up in one arm and Gillian up in the other, with Chase running around him in circles. Lisa met him and brought his chair down. "They've been waiting for you," she said, and winked. "It was hard explaining to them why Uncle Rock couldn't come down to play."

He looked around. "Where's Liz?" he asked.

"Why with you, isn't she?" Lisa said. "I thought the two of you had been holed up in there all afternoon. We haven't seen so much as a stir from your cottage since we came down about forty minutes ago."

"She must have forgotten something and gone back to the grocery store. It's odd that she didn't leave a note though."

"The car's in the garage, Rock. She wouldn't have walked."

Rock started to panic. "Wait a minute," he said, and ran back up to the house. He searched the kitchen, the bedroom and the living room for any sign of a note. When he didn't find one, he walked out on the porch. The shells she had found this morning were spread on the table, but the beach bag she used to put them in was nowhere to be found. The sandals she had been wearing were tucked underneath the table but her flip-flops were gone. Oh God, he prayed silently, please don't let anything happen to her!

He ran back to the beach. By this time, Lisa had told the others and they were waiting for Rock to come back. "She's not here!" he shouted. "I think she's gone out to pick up shells. Some of you go toward the pier. I'll go toward the end of the island."

Lisa started organizing everyone. "Dad, you and Mom go ask Charlie and Macie if they've seen her. Zach, you four go walk up the street toward the gazebo. John and Mike, walk on the beach to the pier." She paused. "And search the walkways and dunes along the way." She turned back to Will. Irene was crying softly. "Don't panic,

Mom! I'm sure she's just resting someplace." Looking at Will more seriously, she said, "Robert and Mark are on the golf course at Sunset Beach so they're not any help, but call them anyway. And call Uncle Joe. Tell him to get down here right away. We may need him more than anyone if she's gone into early labor."

"And call the police," Rock shouted, because deep inside he had a sense of dread that there was more to Liz's disappearance than her going into labor.

Everyone took off, following Lisa's directions. Rock was grateful for her presence of mind. His had flown out the window. "Let's go!," she shouted, and took off running down the beach. He and Allison quickly followed.

***

Liz was in agony when she woke up. She tried to reach for her right hip which was hurting badly, but quickly was reminded that her hands were tied. She managed to get both hands on the spot where the pain was most intense and felt around where it was swollen and bruised. So Tess's kick had missed her stomach where she had been aiming, thank God! Her hands went back to her stomach. There was no movement. She tried to maneuver her hands first to the top of her tummy, then pushing slightly toward the bottom, which always seemed to get the baby to stir around. Still no movement. By now, her back was aching all over and she couldn't get comfortable at all. She couldn't even get up to a sitting position - each time she tried, she slipped back down on the slick hardwood floors. She wondered what time it was. Surely Rock would be awake by now and searching for her. She started crying softly. "Please God....." She could think of nothing else to say.

***

The young boy slipped back in the door quietly. He was alarmed when he found her crying and doubled over with pain. She looked up at him and he could see the pleading in her eyes. Maybe she was having her baby. His mother was pregnant and her baby was due any day now. He had been furious when he found out and he hated his stepfather for doing that to her. But the last few days as he watched the baby move around and heard her talk about the new life growing within her, he had softened a little to it. He had listened through his bedroom wall as she and his stepfather talked about the last minute preparations and what to expect when she went into labor. She had spoken of how bad the pains were when he was born sixteen years earlier. She had also spoken of how hard it had been on him when his father had died, making him think that they cared after all.

Maybe that's what was happening right now to this woman. What would happen to her? Had Tess hurt the baby when she kicked her? He had never seen Ove so furious at Tess. It even shocked Tess when Ove tackled her as she was kicking the poor woman on the floor. He pushed her off balance and instead of the kick landing on the woman's stomach, it hit her hip, but hard. She had moaned and passed out. Tess had reached out to grab her again, but Ove had pulled her away. She had kicked, screamed and scratched, but somehow Ove had managed to get her out the door and put her in her own car. Geir had watched him drive away, with Tess cursing and pulling at Ove's hair.

Then he had walked back inside, not knowing what else to do. He knew he should just get on his bike and go home like Ove had told him to do, but for some reason, he couldn't leave.

Liz watched carefully as the boy paced around the room. He had a large knife - would he hurt her? She tried to move to a better position, but a cramp in her back took her breath away and she cried out in pain.

The boy walked back over to her and bent down. Another cramp hit her and she cried out again.

"I've got to go!" the boy said. He threw down his knife and ran out the door.

Now was her chance. Tess could be coming back any minute and there was pure evil in the girl - more than Liz knew existed in the world. She had to get away - she knew what Tess's intentions were. She would kill her and her baby.

Though the pain was unbearable, she found a determination and strength that she didn't know she possessed. Through the pain, she slid and rolled until she reached the knife that the boy had thrown down. She had watched people free themselves in movies, surely she could cut herself loose. She finally reached the handle of the knife. It was long, more of a machete than a knife. If she could just cut the rope around her ankles, it would relieve some of the pressure from being in such an awkward position - then she would work on her wrists. One thing was certain - she couldn't try for an escape with her ankles bound. The blade was sharp and she was making progress on the threads of the cord. Her hands were numb, but just one more swipe and she would be free. The handle shifted in her hand and she repositioned it so she could continue cutting, but just as she turned the blade once again to the rope, it slipped out of her hands and landed on the inside of her ankle, slicing into it as it came down. She sat helplessly and watched as blood spurted everywhere. She had never seen so much blood - it must have hit an artery. Was this it, then? Would this be the way it would end?

"Your feathers, Lord. Where are they?" Although her hands were numb and her ankle was bleeding profusely, she was able to reach up and pull on the napkin tied around her mouth until it fell in her hands. She tried to wrap the napkin around her bloody ankle to stop the flow, but between her hands being tied and the baby in the middle, she couldn't reach it. She realized that she had no other alternative than to scream, and she did - a bloodcurdling scream that should have shaken the island, she thought when the volume even surprised her. She could only hope that Tess didn't hear it.

CHAPTER 25

"*Therefore pride is their necklace; violence covers them as a garment.*"

- Psalm 73:6 ESV

A half dozen scenarios were playing out in Rock's mind, but the one he kept coming back to was the worst. Why had he not warned Liz about walking on the beach by herself? He hadn't wanted to alarm her, but his failure to tell her all the facts.... He didn't want to think like this. Hopefully, she just walked further than she had intended and stopped to rest. If she had napped with him and then started walking on the beach right before his family went out, then a forty-five minute walk wasn't so bad, was it? But if she had left right after he fell asleep, she could have been gone for over two hours. That was bad.

He tried to pray, he honestly tried, but he could think only of the Bible verse that Liz loved so well. They had talked of how it had comforted her after Ron's death. It was from the 91st Psalm. "*He will cover you with his feathers. He will shelter you with his wings...*" He said it over and over as he ran along the beach, now with Allison and Lisa right behind him.

***

Ove had heard his share of bad language, but the gutteral curses that came out of Tess's mouth were foul. About half of what she said didn't make any sense - just gibberish - but there was no doubt it was profanity at its worst. She made it difficult for him to drive with all the biting, scratching and punching she was doing to him as he tried to make her calm down. He finally grabbed hold of her hair and yanked, holding it tight in his right hand. She screamed, but he just twisted it tighter and she finally stayed still to keep him from hurting her even more.

He knew of a deer hunting cabin about ten miles out of town and that's where he was heading. It was a swampy area and down at the end of a long dirt road lined with trees. He would take her there and hide her keys - throw them in the swamp if he had to. If he could just keep her long enough, someone would find the woman and free her. Hopefully the boy would. When he finally got Tess settled and in the cabin, he would call 911. It was the least he could do for the poor woman.

The road was just ahead. He turned left and picked up his speed. His arm was beginning to cramp and he loosened his hold on Tess's hair just ever so slightly, but it was enough for her to jerk loose. She reached her left leg over and put her foot on top of his on the accelerator. It took him by surprise and he didn't have time to react. With her foot on the accelerator, she gained control of the steering wheel and aimed for a tree on his side of the car. Helplessly he watched as the tree loomed in front of him. The car was headed straight for it. His seat belt was unfastened. He tried to brace himself, but it was too late. He heard glass breaking and felt the impact and lost consciousness before he could feel any pain.

***

Tess was calm as she tried to hitch a ride. In her puffed up image of herself, she felt she was irresistible to men. Now if one would just come by. The only two cars she had seen on the side of the road had been driven by women and they quickly accelerated as they passed her by. She was desperate to get back to the resort. She had unfinished business to take care of. There was nothing rational about her now – she was consumed by the thrill of finishing what she started.

Ove had driven her about ten miles out of town, taking her, he said, to a hiding place where she would be safe, but as they were driving on a small dirt road, she had managed to get her foot on the accelerator and the steering wheel. She sped up and then swerved to the left into a tree, smashing into it on the driver's side. Ove's head hit the glass, but she had braced herself and wasn't hurt bad. The car had hit the tree harder than she had intended. She pulled Ove out onto the ground and tried to start the engine back up, but water spewed from underneath the hood and it wouldn't start. She didn't know how bad he was hurt and she didn't care.

She had grabbed her overnight bag out of the car and changed from her t-shirt and jeans into an off-the-shoulder blouse and shorts. She knew was pretty and knew how to use her looks to her advantage. Her confidence grew along with her delusion of grandeur, but any remnant of rationality she might have once had was gone. Her biggest concern was getting a lift and she soon heard the sound of a vehicle with a loud muffler approaching from behind. She turned around and raised her thumb in the air. A black pick-up truck came to a screeching halt. The driver window rolled down, and two men, both with scraggly beards smiled at her through the opening of the window.

"Hop on in, pretty lady. We'll be glad to give you a ride." For a moment, she felt fear. The feeling was new to her, but it quickly passed. She had the power to handle anything. No dimwitted country hicks were going to frighten her. She opened the back door of the cab and hopped in.

The man in the passenger seat turned around with a big grin on his face. "Fasten your seatbelt honey. We wouldn't want you to get hurt if we have a wreck." He turned to his brother. "And Hoss, maybe you should engage the child safety lock on her side. We sure don't want her to fall out." She tried to open her door to jump out, but Hoss quickly hit the automatic locks and said, "Aw, honey, don't get no bad ideas. You wanted a lift and we're gladly obliging. You remember Rafe here, don't you, young lady? He's my brother."

She shook her head, no.

Rafe spoke up. "Sure you do. You put a little something in our drinks in a bar one night and tempted me with a kiss or two. We went outside with you and in a couple of hours, we woke up beside the dumpster with empty wallets."

She remembered and cursed herself for not recognizing them when they stopped. Rafe turned back around and spoke to his brother, "turn left onto Highway 17, Hoss. This little lady has places she needs to go."

CHAPTER 26

"*The eyes of the Lord are in every place, keeping watch on the evil and the good.*"

- Proverbs 15:3 ESV

Rock was worried. They should have seen Liz by now. They had passed what the detective had called the Devil's Footpath and and the beached sailboats. They were closing in on the beach entrance to the resort when a flash of orange in the sea oats up ahead caught his eye. Her beach bag! He called out to his sisters and tried to pick up speed. A cramp in his leg had slowed him down, but he kept going. Again, he hoped that she had just tired out and would be sitting at the top of the stairs waiting for him. As he grew closer, there were still no signs of her and his hope wavered. He reached the stairs and someone shouted at him from above. A boy, not much younger than Zachary was at the top of the stairs motioning for him to come up. Rock ran up the stairs, followed closely by Allison and Lisa. The boy was stuttering and Rock had a hard time making out what he was saying, but when he neared the top, the boy had calmed down somewhat.

"A lady," he shouted. "I think she's having a baby." He motioned for Rock to follow. Just then a scream filled the air, and he stopped dead in his tracks.

Could that be Liz? Such a scream couldn't possibly belong to his calm and quiet wife..., could it? The boy was running up the steps of a building much larger than the houses around it. Rock stopped on the steps to catch his breath, but the boy motioned from the door.

"Quick - inside," he said.

Could it be a trap? He turned back to his sisters who were about 20 feet behind.

"Lisa," he said. "Call Mom and Dad and tell them to get some help out here. I don't know if we need the police or an ambulance - get both! I'm going inside. If I don't come right back out, run for help."

Rock had decided that no matter what awaited him inside, if Liz was in there, he was going to be with her. He had seen the boy go through an entrance from the main room to another room to the left. He followed, and the sight before him shocked him to the core. Liz was huddled on the floor and the boy was bending down to her with a knife in his hands. Blood was everywhere. His first reaction was to rush the boy to knock him down, but Liz saw his intentions and yelled, "Rock! Stop! He's just cutting me loose." The boy had already cut her feet and hands free when Rock reached her. When he saw the cut on her ankle, Geir reached into the cabinet drawer and pulled out more napkins and handed them to Rock.

"Here's something to stop the bleeding," he said. When Rock looked at him accusingly, the boy said, "I didn't cut her," and stepped away.

"He's right. He didn't," Liz said. "I cut myself when I was trying to get loose." She was flexing her wrists trying to get her circulation flowing. "Rock, why is it bleeding so much? I'm so glad you're here."

The sound of several sirens filled the air.

Rock tightened the napkin above her ankle to make a tourniquet. Then he sat on the floor holding her closely in his arms and rocking her back and forth. All the tears she had tried to hold back came flooding forth. All the worry he had been feeling brought tears to his eyes too, but he wouldn't let them fall. He had to be strong for Liz.

Lisa and Allison tentatively stuck their heads around the corner and when they saw Rock was in no danger they came in. Lisa was the first to faint at the sight of blood, followed quickly by Allison.

"A lot of help you are," Rock said to the limp sisters who didn't hear him. He turned to the boy who was also sitting on the floor with his head between his hands. "We're going to need three ambulances, maybe four, depending on how you're feeling," he said.

"I don't need an ambulance," he said in a wistful voice. "I n-n-need my Mama." He paused and looked up. "And maybe a lawyer...."

***

The West End Winter Resort was crawling with emergency vehicles. Charlie was later to be heard saying that he thought the whole dad-burned resort had gone up in flames. "Wouldn't have bothered me none," he said, "those high-falutin' folks think they own the island."

Most of the vehicles seemed to come in pairs; two rescue vans, two county sheriff's deputies, two of the Island Police squad cars, and one lone fire truck lined up in the circular driveway of the club house. Uncle Joe had arrived just ahead of them and was parked at the back entrance. Joe was inside with Liz and Rock.

The rescue attendants had moved Allison and Lisa to the dining room chairs and made sure their heads were lower than their knees. They soon felt revived enough to stand up. "If the sight of blood bothers you, I would suggest you go out of the room, ladies," one of them said. The sisters didn't object and hurried out to join the rest of the family outside on the deck.

Irene was crying as they waited for someone to come out and give them more information. She threw her arms around Lisa and then Allison as they came down the steps. The girls filled them in on what they had seen, leaving out the worst of it for Irene's sake.

"Poor Liz! Do you think she'll be okay?" she asked her husband.

Will was beginning to lose patience with his wife. He was worried too, and Irene's theatrics were about to put him over the edge. "Irene, I've told you that I don't know any more than you. Joe is in there with her now. I trust him... and I trust the Lord.

"Oh, Will - I'm so scared."

He put his arm around her and patted her on the back. "Me too, Irene, but she'll be alright."

"I hope so." She suddenly put her hand over her heart. "I think I'm having a heart attack!"

Will looked at her but knew that a bit of drama was one of her ways of handling stressful situations.

"Well, Irene, honey. You've come to the right place to have one," he said. "There's two rescue workers right here." He took a step toward the attendant. "I'll go see...."

She glared at him. "Will, you never take me seriously. One of these days I'm just going to drop over dead when I'm having one of these spells and you'll be sorry you didn't listen to me." She blew her nose on a tissue the deputy had given her earlier, and then sighed. "Oh, I'm okay... I'm sure it's just the stress. You know I don't handle stress well."

Will reached over and held her in his arms. "I know dear. I know."

Allison exchanged glances with her father and smiled.

***

Joe had brought his medical kit and was examining Liz. They had pulled one of the sofas from the club's gathering room into the dining hall to make her more comfortable. When the medics were satisfied that the blood flow had stopped, they stood back to give him some space after he let them know he was the medical doctor in charge of her health and for now, he needed to see about the baby. He said it in a friendly but precise tone of voice and Rock noticed that they all seemed respectful of his title.

Rock was pacing back and forth. "Slow down, Rock. You're making me nervous," Liz said with a faint smile. He couldn't slow down. His mind hadn't stopped swirling since Liz told him the baby had stopped moving. He was worried sick, for Liz and for the baby. He finally stopped and looked on as his uncle kneeled beside Liz with his stethoscope, listening carefully for the baby's heartbeat.

Finally, after gently pushing on her abdomen, he turned around to Rock. "Come on over here, Rock. I want both of you to hear me at the same time." At Rock's terrified expression, he hastened to tell him not to worry.

"Liz has lost a lot of blood from her cut," he said. "Peripheral venous pressure in a pregnant woman tends to be higher in the lower extremities...

"Wait, talk to us in terms we can understand. I'm not thinking very straight right now anyway."

"I don't think any of us are, Rock," Joe said. "I'm sorry, I got carried away. Let's try again. The veins in the legs of a pregnant woman are under more pressure than normal because of the compression by the uterus on the large vein that carries blood from the lower body to the heart. That's why a lot of women have varicose veins during a pregnancy. It's also why lacerations on the lower body, the legs especially, bleed so profusely."

"But what's going to happen?" Rock and Liz said at the exact same time.

"I think a unit of blood is in order. Liz, your blood pressure is low, but the baby's heartbeat is strong. The reason you're not feeling any movement is because he's a good little chap and is conserving his energy until your blood pressure stabilizes. I'm hoping this will continue. You took quite a jolt, didn't you?"

Liz nodded. Rock worried.

Joe packed up his instruments in his bag. "By the way, what's your blood type?"

She closed her eyes for a moment and then looked up at him. "B negative," she said with her face in a grimace.

"Yikes," he said, "one of the rarest types. I just hope it's available at the hospital." He motioned to the rescue medics. "And where is the nearest hospital?"

"Comer General, it's about six miles from here."

"Thanks. Please take her there and keep checking her blood pressure. I know I don't need to tell you that - you guys know the ropes. Her husband will be riding with her. I'll take my car and I'll call ahead to make sure they'll allow outside physicians in their facility. He paused for a minute. "We need to hurry."

One of the medics spoke up. "I don't think it will be a problem. But if it is, my wife's father is the hospital administrator. He can pull a few strings." He turned to the other medic. "I'll go get the stretcher. You stay here with her."

Rock walked outside to try and reassure his family. His mother caught him by the hand and gave him a hug. "Don't worry," he told them. There was no use for them to worry - he was doing enough of it for all of them. He needed to keep them calm - his mom would go into a tizzy. Acting much more assured than he felt, he spoke again. "Joe thinks she'll be fine - the baby too. She's lost a lot of blood from cutting herself with the knife she was trying to use to get free, so they'll be giving her a unit of blood if the hospital has her type. Any of you have B negative?"

One of the sheriff's deputies raised his hand. "I do! And I don't mind giving it. I get called all the time because mine's rare. I think I've given at least three gallons in my lifetime."

Joe had come out and heard the conversation. "Can you ride with me, just in case we need for you to donate?"

The other deputy spoke up. "Why don't we give you an escort?" It'll get you there early to make the arrangements. Beach Rescue has its own sirens so they'll have no problems. We need to be there anyway to finish filling out our report."

Joe got in his car and rolled the window down. "I'm ready - let's get going."

Rock watched as Joe pulled away behind the deputies' car with lights flashing and sirens blaring. The sound filled him with worry all over again. He looked at his watch. They should be bringing Liz out shortly. Then, turning back to the doorway, he saw Detective Garrett walking his way and felt a flash of anger.

"Reverend Clark, I wish all the best for your wife and your baby," he said. Rock just nodded curtly. He tried to squelch his feelings of anger and annoyance that the police had seemed to drop the ball in the other kidnapping. It seemed to him that an arrest should have been made by now, or at least some surveillance at the site where it happened. If they had done their jobs, Liz's kidnapping could have been prevented.

As if he knew what Rock was thinking, the detective looked embarrassed. "We didn't have much to go on in Mr. Peterson's case." He looked down at his feet, then back up at Rock. "To tell you the truth, I didn't take it nearly serious enough. I was convinced it was a bad prank played by some college students that had been down here for a few days celebrating the end of their junior year. The boys had already gotten in some trouble - drinking and disturbing the peace, destroying personal property, and the like. I had called the homeowner of the house they were renting the day before the kidnapping. He gave them one more night and they were told they had to leave the next day. I went by the house after you found Mr. Peterson and since they were gone, I figured they had just put on one more revengeful fling before they left. Peterson was okay, the kids were gone and nothing else was happening, so we pulled surveillance off. That was a mistake."

Rock tried to absorb it all, but finally just shook his head. He was just glad that the Park Place Police were not this incompetent. He looked up and saw they were finally coming out with Liz. She looked so pale. He didn't have time to stand there talking. He hated to be rude, but he ignored the detective and started to go to Liz.

"You can ride in the front with the driver if you want to," the medic said. "It will be more comfortable."

"I'll ride back here with my wife if it's not against the rules."

"It's not. Just give us a minute to hook up the IV and we'll get started."

"Reverend Clark?" It was Detective Garrett again. "I'm really sorry that this has happened. We know who we're looking for now. The boy here has been very cooperative. I promise we'll find them."

Rock's attitude softened when he saw the look of remorse on the detective's face. "I'm sure you will," he said. "You guys have a tough job to do every day, and you're only human just like the rest of us. Sometimes we judge situations right and sometimes we're wrong. We just do the best we can." There, he'd said it. Now if he could really mean it.

The detective looked at him with relief. "Thank you for putting my mind at ease. Good luck and God bless."

The medic in the back snapped Liz in place. "We're ready. Hop in." Rock got in the back and as he found his seat, the back door started automatically closing. "Ready to roll," the medic shouted to the front of the van.

The Clark family stood and watched helplessly as the lights flashed and the siren sounded. Irene was crying. "Will, tell me again they'll be okay." She looked up into her husband's eyes.

"They'll be okay, Irene." His voice was unconvincing, but he tried to put up a good front.

The boy sat silently on the bottom step with Detective Garrett standing close by. An occasional sob was the only sound he made. John, who had once worked with troubled youth went and sat beside him. "What's your name, son?"

"M-M-Marcus."

He stutters, John thought. Just a young kid who's scared half to death and stutters. "Can I call someone for you, Marcus?" He gave him a pat on the back.

"Th-they've already called my Mama. She's going to meet us at the police station." The sobbing had stopped but an occasional snuffle and catch of his breath made John remember that this was just a child. "Sh-she's going to hate me. I've given her nothing but grief since Daddy died."

"She's not going to hate you. I'm a parent too and I could never hate my children. I may want to burn their backsides once in a while, but it's just about impossible to hate your own child. Do you have other family?"

"Just a sister - she's twelve." He shuffled his feet around on the concrete step. "And my step-father. And another baby on the way." He looked miserable, but John knew he should keep him talking so he wouldn't worry himself so.

"Can I call your step-father? Sometimes men are better at dealing with boys getting into trouble. Do you have a good relationship with him?"

"No!" The boy said it so adamantly that John wondered what kind of man this stepfather was.

"I-If anyone has a reason to hate me, it's him. I've done everything I could to break up their marriage." He rubbed his eyes with both hands, and looked off in the distance. "It's not that he's done anything b-bad to me," he said. "He keeps trying, but I don't want any part of it. M-my daddy loved mama and she shouldn't have married again. And now, having a baby - it's just wrong."

"I know it's hard for you to understand, but it was equally as hard on your mother to lose her husband as it was for you to lose your daddy - maybe harder." The boy looked at him skeptically, but John continued. "Sometimes the loneliness is just too much - or the financial hardships from losing the spouse's salary - or all the better, they fall in love again. There are lots of reasons people marry again after the one they love has died, but it's her decision and it's done. I hope you can find it in your heart to respect that. It'll make things easier for you."

Detective Garrett watched as the two of them talked. He spoke to Robert who had been standing in the crowd. "These Clark men are a forgiving lot. I wonder what's their secret?"

Robert looked at his wife's family still gathered there and was proud. "God," he said.

CHAPTER 27

"*A*re not two sparrows sold for a cent? And yet not one of them will fall to the ground apart from your Father. But the very hairs of your head are all numbered. So do not fear; you are more valuable than many sparrows.*"

For Rock, the ambulance ride seemed to take forever, when in fact, the report filed by the medics later that afternoon listed it as only eighteen minutes from start to finish. Liz's blood pressure dropped to a dangerous level, but the medic added a medication to the drip line and it was finally stable by the time they pulled into the Emergency Room entrance.

The hospital staff was waiting and it took no time at all to get her in. By the time Rock finished the paperwork, she was already in a critical care room. When Rock became alarmed at the term critical care, Joe explained that it was basically the same as what some hospitals call ICU – intensive care. His explanation didn't relieve Rock's fears at all.

The hospital allowed Joe to be a consultant MD to the hospital staff doctor who was assigned to her. As Joe had feared, Liz's blood type was not in the hospital's supply. The deputy's blood type was already on file at the hospital, so as soon as they matched it with his identity and her type, they put him on a gurney and drew a unit of blood. Within thirty minutes, a fresh pint of B negative was flowing into Liz's veins.

Rock wasn't allowed in the room so he walked to the waiting room where his mother and sisters stood vigil. Mike was there too. He took one look at Rock and saw that he was struggling to keep up appearances, so he took him by the arm and led him out into the hallway. "Let's go downstairs to the chapel," he said.

"Let me make a couple of phone calls first." He used his cell phone to call Eleanor, Liz's mother.

"Do you think I should fly or drive?" she asked.

"By the time you drive to the airport and then have to rent a car once you get to Wilmington, you could probably already be here by car," he told her. "They have everything under control, so don't speed," he told her, wondering himself if what he was telling her was true.

He called Reva next and asked her to get the phone tree in operation to let everyone know to pray. He was glad to hear her voice. In emergency situations, Reva was always a calming influence for him and he felt better after talking with her.

When he and Mike finally got to the chapel, his father and John were there already on bended knee at the alter. He knelt down beside his father and was grateful when Mike's booming voice started talking to God, lifting up Liz and their little boy in prayer. He finally felt at peace after such a tumultuous day.

They left the chapel and took the elevator upstairs to the waiting room where they found the sheriff and the chief of police waiting for them. The sheriff looked at each of the men and then turned his attention back to Rock. "You're Reverend Clark, I take it?"

Rock smiled. "Yes, but there's three of us who are Reverend Clark," he said, pointing to Mike and John. "I'm Rock Clark - just call me Rock."

"So it runs in the family?" The sheriff, who Rock thought must be in his early sixties held out his hand. "I'm Matt Baker, the county sheriff, and you can call me Matt... or Baker which is what most people call me."

"Are you here to give us some information on who did this?" Rock asked.

"Yes, and I think you'll be glad to know we have the other two suspects in custody. One of them is being treated here at the hospital. The other is at the detention center still being questioned. They're waiting for a court appointed lawyer."

Rock looked around when he heard the door to the waiting room open, hoping it was a nurse telling him he could see Liz. It was just Allison, returning with two cups of coffee, handing one to their mom and the other to their dad.

Sheriff Baker waited until he turned back to face him.

"You'll have to excuse me. I'm a little distracted," Rock said.

"Understandably," the sheriff responded.

"I'm glad to know they're off the streets and not out hurting someone else. Who are they....and why Liz?" He noticed the whole family trying to hear. "Let's go sit with my family so they'll all know what's going on. It's better to hear it from you."

"Sure. Who they are first, then we'll get to your other question."

Rock pulled two chairs so he and the sheriff would be in front of the rest of the family. The family was attentive as the sheriff told about Ove, whose real name was Johnny Lewis, nineteen years old and a product of a broken family, raised most of the time by his grandmother," the sheriff said. "This is a poor county - hard to find work except during the summer tourist season - the rest of the time the job pickings are slim. The kids who can afford to go off to college don't usually come back - there's just nothing to hold them here - no work. He works as a mechanic for a local guy's auto repair shop. The work isn't steady, but it's enough for him to rent a singlewide mobile home in a rundown trailer park. Apparently, he scrapes by."

"He's got a rap sheet, nothing major, stealing groceries, gas. One of the victims was a small grocer who knows the grandmother so he dropped the charges. Then he got caught selling marijuana, not a large amount, but the prosecution arranged a plea deal in exchange for information which helped bring about the arrest of a big time drug dealer, a major supplier in the Wilmington area. With the plea deal, Johnny didn't have to serve time."

"How did he get involved with the cult?" Rock wanted to know how much under the spell this guy was.

"Well, that brings us to the girl, who by the way is a piece of work! We tried to interview her about thirty minutes ago. I've seen mean and I've seen evil during my time in law enforcement, but I've never seen anything like her. That girl has sold her soul to the devil, if there's any such thing."

Rock nodded. "There is."

"She's from the DC area. Her parents are wealthy and gave her everything she ever asked for. I talked with them about thirty minutes ago. When I told them what she had done, they were shocked. She's been in trouble before and they've always come to her rescue. They're not going to do it this time. She's on her own." He pushed his chair back and reached into his briefcase to retrieve a notebook and look at his notes.

She calls herself Tess, but her real name is Betsy McCall - ironic, isn't it. Betsy McCall, like the paperdoll cutouts from the 1950's McCall magazines." He looked at Rock, but didn't get a reaction. "You're too young to know about Betsy McCall. My sisters couldn't wait to get that magazine every month." He turned to Irene. "Do you remember?" She nodded her head.

"She's twenty-two - went to prison about two years ago and never went back home when she got out. She's been involved in satanic cults up and down the eastern seaboard, starting in the Baltimore area. She admitted she'd always wanted to be a leader of an occult herself, so she came down here and recruited these two local boys. She claims that Johnny was under her spell and she's convinced that no man can resist her evil charms - very delusional, and quite proud of it."

Rock felt sick to his stomach. To think that this much evil had been so close to Liz. He shuddered to think what could have happened. "Was Johnny with her when you found her?"

"No. By this time, Johnny and the other boy, Marcus, had both, on their own begun to be frightened of Tess. I interviewed both of them, separately, and their stories meshed." He stopped, rubbed his hand across his brow and looked at Rock with a serious expression. "These boys, especially Johnny, saved your baby's life, and more than likely your wife's life too, depending on what the girl's plans were for her. She wouldn't say."

The whole room became quiet and everyone's attention was on Sheriff Baker. He looked at Rock intently. "Yes, you heard right. She succeeded in kicking your wife on the hip, but she was aiming for the baby, and if Johnny hadn't intervened and tackled her, I don't know how far she would have gone."

Rock felt an uncontrollable rage. His heart was racing and he knew that if the girl, Tess had been within reach, he would have strangled her. It was a feeling so new to him, that it frightened him at what he would be capable of doing to this woman if she had succeeded in taking the life of Liz or the baby. And they still were not out of the woods. He got up from his chair and walked to the door. He needed desperately to see Liz.

John was as shocked as anyone at what the sheriff had told them. He could see what a profound effect this news was having on his nephew, and got up and followed him out the door. Rock was just standing in the hallway looking lost. John walked up behind him and put his hands on his shoulders. "Are you okay?"

He turned around. "John, you don't even want to know what I'm thinking," he said. "It scares even me. I've got to get a grip on myself."

"You know, sometimes it's good to just go ahead and get the anger out in the open, Rock. We men of the cloth are no different than anyone else when it comes to our families. It's okay to be mad, it's okay to want to lash out and hurt someone like this Tess. You know, I don't even like to say her name - Betsy, Tess - whatever it is, this is evil personified, and it's okay to be angry with evil."

Rock breathed a sigh of relief. "You don't know how much I needed to hear that. I just wanted to.., well, just say a prayer for me, John. I know it will do me no good to fight evil with evil, but I just hope she gets what she deserves."

"She will. From what Sheriff Baker is saying, it looks like she'll be charged with kidnapping and attempted murder. I don't think there'll be any light sentences handed out for either of those charges."

"You know, that's something we need to preach on more often – spiritual warfare. The devil is always looking for a door to open, an empty mind, seeking something other than God's word. We have to prepare our kids."

John nodded. "Yes we do." He looked down at his watch. "I wonder what's taking my brother, the doctor so long?"

As if on cue, Joe walked out of the critical care room and shut the door. He was all smiles. "I've ordered quiet and bedrest for your wife, but she told me she's not going to settle down until she sees you." He turned to John. "I wonder what that beautiful woman in there sees in this knucklehead nephew of ours?"

"She sees someone who's head over heels for her, quite probably," John said. "Have you ever heard of being blinded by love?" They both laughed.

"How is she Uncle Joe? And the baby, is he going to be okay?"

"Let's go see for ourselves," he said, and led Rock into the room.

Liz smiled when she saw Rock. "I was afraid you had abandoned me!" He took two strides and was by her bedside. He started to bend down to hug her, but looked at Joe. Joe nodded his head and he hugged her gently.

"Go ahead, she won't break," Joe said. "She and the baby seem to be fine. I ordered an ultrasound and it shows clearly the baby is not in distress right now. Liz has the pictures - she'll show you. That little fellow is taking up all the space in there. The cervix has dilated about three centimeters so If I had to make a guess, I would say he'll be making his grand entrance in about two weeks, a week or so earlier than the due date. But even with all my experience, your guess is as good as mine - babies come when they're good and ready. The jolt she took when she was pushed around is somewhat of a concern, but I'm going to call Dr. Anderson and ask him to follow up when you get back home."

Rock smoothed her hair gently with his hand. "How do you feel?"

"I feel fine except for my hip. I have a feeling I'm going to have a doozy of a bruise."

Rock looked at Joe. "There's nothing broken, Rock. But there will be a bruise. We can be thankful that the girl had on soft toed shoes instead of cowboy boots, though."

The image of Liz lying on the floor scared and being kicked around made him cringe. He took her by the hand. "Liz, I'm so sorry I wasn't there to protect you." He looked deep into her eyes.

Her lip trembled for a minute, but then smiled. "You didn't know, Rock. It was stupid for me to leave and not write you a note. But God was there - He protected me. I quoted part of the twenty-third Psalm the whole while she was dragging me up to the clubhouse. *Yea, though I walk through the valley of the shadow of death, I will fear no evil: for thou art with me, thy rod and thy staff, they comfort me...* You know, I could feel His presence walking right along beside me."

"He did protect you. It could have been so much worse."

Liz yawned. "Did you call my mother?"

"Yes, I forgot to tell you. She's driving up." He looked at his watch. "She should be here soon."

The ultrasound images were from the newest technology and Rock was amazed by them. "I feel like I'm looking at a real baby," he said.

"You are, you silly goose. What did you think he was going to be, a pretend baby."

Rock laughed. "You know what I mean. I just didn't expect these images to be so clear. The last ones back home were good, but nothing like this!"

"They have state of the art equipment here - probably more advanced than in your doctor's office," Joe said.

"We gave her something to make her rest - she's had quite an ordeal today, so I'm going to the waiting room to see the family. Stay as long as you like."

Rock held her hand until the medication took effect and she drifted off to sleep. He sat in the chair and looked at his sweet and spirited wife and thanked God that He had protected her and the baby. He put his hand on her stomach and was rewarded with a swift kick. "That's my boy!" he said.

Joe stuck his head back in the room. "They're all waiting for you," he said. "I didn't tell them much - just told them you would be out shortly to let them know how she's doing."

After his family was all satisfied that Liz was okay, they slowly started drifting out of the waiting room to make their way back to the beach houses. "The kids are all hungry," Lisa said. "They're threatening Zach and Laurie with mutiny. I promised to pick up pizzas on the way home. It was Joe's night to cook and it's 8 o'clock already. And oh, by the way Rock, you and Liz are off the hook for cooking tomorrow night."

"Thanks, Sis. I don't think you would want to eat my cooking, but the food's in the refrigerator if anyone wants to volunteer to cook it."

"Since we are all getting off light tonight, we'll cook tomorrow night. But I may have to badger Liz tomorrow for her recipe."

CHAPTER 28

"*B*ut *every man is tested when he is turned out of the right way by the attraction of his desire. Then when its time comes, desire gives birth to sin; and sin, when it is of full growth, gives birth to death. Do not be turned from the right way, dear brothers.*"

- James 1:14-16 BBE

Rock was surprised to see that Sheriff Baker was still in the waiting room. The Police Chief had gone home. Rock walked over and sat down. "I'm just curious, Matt. How did you find them and make the arrest so quickly?"

"Well, this is where it gets interesting and the beginning of the unraveling of Tess. Like I said earlier, she was on a rampage, but Johnny somehow got her out of the building and away from your wife. He physically carried her to the car and drove her away from there. She protested and scratched, bit and hit him, but he managed to get her about ten miles out of town and was planning to leave her in a deer hunter's cabin he knew of out in the woods, then go back and check on your wife."

"Her name is Liz," Rock said.

"Thank you - he was going back to check on Liz, but Tess managed to take control of the steering wheel and rammed them into a tree. He hit his head on the windshield and it knocked him out. She pushed him out of the car and tried to drive, but it wouldn't run."

"Wow, she was determined wasn't she?"

"Well, from what I've heard, when the devil takes hold of a person, he don't easily let go."

Rock was impressed with his insight. "You're right, Matt. And it sounds like she was definitely possessed."

"But this is where some of her old mistakes came back to haunt her. By her own admission, she started walking back and if the right person had given her a ride, she would have gone back to the clubhouse - she was that determined."

Rock shook his head.

"I know Rock, it's beyond understanding. But this is the best part. This Tess, she messed with the wrong people when she scammed the Hatley brothers a while back. Rafe and Hoss Hatley are two good ole' boys from the green swamp country, about as far back in the swamps as you can go without getting eaten by an alligator."

Rock smiled, and the sheriff continued.

"Rafe and Hoss just happened to be driving down this same road where she was walking. They recognized her and picked her up. She found them somewhat frightening, but who wouldn't? Long beards and somewhat smelly - they work in a hog parlor."

Rock envisioned what they must have looked like and laughed.

"But these two boys had been listening to the police scanner and by that time, we had an alert out on Tess and Johnny. They brought her straight to our department headquarters and turned her in. I was there, sitting at my desk when they brought her in. I actually think she was relieved to be going to jail rather than having to stay with the Hatley brothers."

He had been laughing while telling the story, but all of a sudden he became serious. He looked Rock straight in the face. "Reverend Clark..." Seeing Rock's look and arched eyebrow, he shifted in his chair and corrected himself. "Rock, I want you to be assured that they're going to pay for what they've done, especially the girl, Tess. For some reason, I can't even say her name without wanting to throw up."

"That's what my uncle said."

"With what Johnny and that kid did to help your wife ‑ to help Liz, they'll get off lighter, but this girl is going to serve some serious time for what she's done. I'll see to it."

"I hope so," Rock said. "How is Johnny? Is he still in the hospital?"

"Yes, he's officially under arrest, but he'll be kept here overnight for observation. He took quite a knock on the head ‑ a concussion, the emergency room doctor said."

"I want to go see him and thank him for what he did for Liz."

"That'll be fine. I'll go up with you; then I've got to get back to the office. You know, from my experience, it's usually the kids who are lost and have no direction, who end up getting in trouble. I wish there was funding for an athletic center or something in this county to give them something to do."

"There's a need for that everywhere," Rock said. "And if we could just get them in church...."

CHAPTER 29

"*He has delivered us from the power of darkness and conveyed us into the kingdom of the Son of His love.*"

- Colossians 1:13 NKJV

Johnny Lewis was asleep when they walked in the room. Rock had asked the deputy standing guard outside the room if there had been anyone in to see him.

"Not a soul, and it's not likely that he'll have visitors either. As a matter of fact, I don't even know who to call except maybe his grandmother and she doesn't need to burdened by this."

"Doesn't he have other family?"

"Well, yes - I know his family. I also know where his no-good daddy is but we didn't call him. He would only show up here drunk, but he hasn't seen the kid in years anyway. His mom is the kind that goes from one man to another - anyone as long as she doesn't have to pay rent. His grandmother is the only one who's ever played an active role in his life but she lives way up in Leland and doesn't drive."

"Let's go in and talk to him." He knocked softly and then pushed the door open. Sheriff Baker closed it behind them. The sound of the door closing startled Johnny. His whole body jerked and there was raw fear in his eyes when he opened them. He seemed to be relieved when he saw Rock and the sheriff. "I was dreaming that

Tess was coming after me with the boy's big knife," he said. He looked at the sheriff. "You did say she's locked up, didn't you?"

"Yes, you don't need to worry about her."

He turned back to Rock and then turned his gaze to the wall. He seemed reluctant to talk - almost embarrassed, but he finally looked Rock in the eye and spoke. "Is your wife going to be okay?"

Rock looked at him, trying to gauge his motive but decided he looked genuinely concerned. "She is - and the baby too. I want to thank you for what you did in the clubhouse to protect the baby - and my wife."

He shook his head as if trying to get the afternoon's happenings out of his mind. "It was stupid of me to get mixed up with Tess to begin with. She made herself out to be sweet in the beginning and I fell hard for her. But then... well, it was little things at first, like building a fire out there in the dunes. Then she brought a live chicken to kill - a sacrifice she said. It was sort of a lark at first, I didn't have anything else to do and I couldn't say no to her. I just got caught up into it. But last summer she stole a small dog. I like dogs and it about turned my stomach when I saw what she was going to do with it. I tried to talk her out of it, but she turned her knife on me. That's when I started being afraid of her, but I just couldn't break away. Later she told me she was sorry and that she wouldn't have hurt me with the knife, but I didn't trust her much after that. Last fall, she just up and disappeared. She stayed gone for several months and I didn't hear a word from her. I was glad - I felt like I had finally broken away from her spell. But in March, she showed up again, and it wasn't long before she started showing up with the boy - Geiv she called him, but his real name is Marcus as I'm sure you know by now."

He quit talking for a while, and pressed his hand to the front of his head. "This is a doozy of a headache."

"You need to get your rest. We'll go now." Rock turned toward the door.

"No, I need to tell you this." He looked pleadingly at Rock. "So you'll understand." Rock knew that no matter what he said, he would never understand, but he stopped to hear him out.

"You pretty much know the rest of the story, or at least what happened to the poor man that came down the Devil's Footpath. She stole a couple more chickens before that and had the boy under her spell too. He would cut the heads off with that huge machete he carries." He shook his head as if trying to get the images out of his mind. "I still can't believe I ever got involved with that mumbo jumbo stuff."

Rock listened as he told about Tess watching from the boardwalk as they rescued Peterson, and how she told him to 'take care' of Peterson, but he wouldn't do it.

"She blamed you and those kids for nosing around and finding the man. I don't know what her plans for him were, and I don't want to know, but for some reason it made her furious with you that you found him and when she heard you were a preacher, it made her worse. She told us she was going to make you pay. By this time I didn't know what to do. I wanted to be rid of her, but she knew where to find me. I even went up to Leland and spent a night with my grandma, but when I got back yesterday, she called me and asked me to meet her at the clubhouse, and like an idiot, I did."

"I'm glad you did," Rock said. "I shudder to think what would have happened to Liz if you hadn't been there."

"It wouldn't have been good." He looked at Rock. "I guess that's what Granny means by someone being at the right place at the right time, ain't it?"

"I think your Granny hit the nail on the head," he said. "Have you ever heard about God using evil to accomplish something good?"

The boy looked away, embarrassed, but Rock continued. "In the Bible, Joseph's brothers sold him into slavery because they were jealous of him. But eventually Joseph found favor from the pharaoh in the land where he was enslaved, by interpreting his dreams. The dream was of a great famine to come. The pharaoh put him in charge of the storage and distribution of food to save up for the famine and when it came, they were ready. Even his brothers came to beg for food and he told them in Genesis 50:20, *You intended to harm me, but God intended it for good to accomplish what is now being done, the saving of many lives.*"

Johnny looked at him skeptically. "What does that have to do with me?"

Rock smiled. "It means that God used the evil that the brothers meant for Joseph to save people from starving during the famine." He looked at Johnny to see if he understood. He couldn't be sure, but he had a feeling it would stay with him. "You can read the whole story in Genesis, and in your case, even through all this evil, God used you to save my wife and my baby. It could be that He's even using it to save you."

"Huh!" he said. "I don't know about all that stuff. You sound too much like my Granny."

Rock looked at Sheriff Baker, then back at the boy. "Your Granny sounds like a pretty wise woman," he said.

The sheriff nodded. "And I think we're on to something," he said. "If Johnny's able to get probation instead of a jail sentence, I'm thinking that one of the terms of his probation could be to spend a year with Granny, if she'll have him, that is."

"Oh no," Johnny groaned. "She'll have me alright. She'd like nothin' better than to get her Bible thumpin' paws on me."

Rock had one more concern and knew he may as well just come out and say it. The boy was going to need some spiritual guidance if this had gone too far. "Johnny, just how deep did you get in this devil worshiping business?"

Johnny started to speak, then closed his mouth and didn't say anything for a minute. Uh oh, I've gone too far too quickly, Rock thought. I should have waited. But then the boy spoke.

"I started to say not at all - that I didn't want anything to do with worshipping the devil. But now I think about how I practically worshiped Tess and how she told me I was under her spell. I guess she was right. Does that mean I'm just as evil?"

Rock's heart sank. "How do you feel about her now?"

"I hate everything about her!"

It was a pretty strong statement but Rock was relieved that he seemed to have been more focused on the girl rather than what she worshipped. Now even that infatuation was over.

"That's a big first step." He picked up the Bible that was placed in the hospital room by the Gideons. Johnny rolled his eyes, but stayed attentive.

"Here's what I was looking for. It's from the 4th chapter of James, verses 7 and 8." The print was small, so he pulled out his reading glasses. "*Therefore submit to God. Resist the devil and he will flee from you. Draw near to God and He will draw near to you.*" He handed the Bible to Johnny. "James is a good place to start," he said. "Then go from there to John. Keep reading and even your Bible thumpin' Granny, as you call her, will be impressed."

Johnny laughed, then grew serious. "She's all I've got, Granny is. She's so good and I've worried her to death. How did I ever get so off course - I just don't know."

Rock was surprised at his openness. It sounded like he really wanted to change direction. "We get to choose what paths we take in life, Johnny. You've been choosing the wrong ones. Just like that place you call the Devil's Footpath - it's filled with gnarled trees, prickly bushes and all the things you don't want to get into. But there are better paths to the sea - straight paths or meandering paths, but smoother and much more pleasant to follow. It's your choice, Johnny. So many paths, so many directions and I pray that you'll start following the right one."

The door opened and a nurse walked in with a tray of food. "It's a little late for dinner, but I saw on your chart that you haven't eaten yet."

Sheriff Baker stepped aside so she could slide the tray on the table. "We'd better go and let Johnny get some food and some rest."

"Granny would have said grace," the boy spoke sheepishly from the bed.

Rock bowed his head and prayed. As they went out into the hallway, Rock stopped and spoke to the deputy. "I think you should call his grandmother. She'll want to know and he's going to need her."

"I'll do it," he said. "I think I can even arrange for someone to pick her up tomorrow and get her down here."

***

Rock said goodnight to Sheriff Baker and was on his way to Liz's room when he saw her mom get off the elevator. "Eleanor," he called out to her and made his way to greet her.

"Rock, how is she? I've been worried sick all the way up here."

He took her by the arm. "She and the baby are both fine now. I'll take you down to her room. She was in good spirits when I left her about twenty minutes ago."

"You'll have to tell me all about it, but I want to see her first. You know how we mothers are. We want to see for ourselves."

Rock laughed. "I'm going to be finding all about how you mothers are in about two weeks."

"That soon?" she asked.

"Apparently it's all a guessing game, but yes, Uncle Joe, who's been her attending physician here thinks so."

She looked at him questioningly. "Your Uncle Joe?"

"I know, it's confusing. I'll fill you in later. Here's her room." Rock walked in first, followed by Eleanor. Liz was asleep. He walked to the side of her bed. "Honey, your mom's here."

She opened her eyes and looked from him to her mother. Her bottom lip started trembling, then she burst out in tears.

Rock looked baffled. "Liz, what's wrong?" he asked.

Eleanor pushed past him. "She just wants her Mama," Eleanor said.

Liz nodded her head, still sobbing. "Mama, I'm so glad you're here!"

Rock shook his head, muttering, "I don't understand. She was fine just a few minutes ago." Neither of them paid him any attention. "Uh, I'll just go outside now and leave you two alone." Still no response. It must be a mother thing, he said to himself and walked outside into the hallway.

He pouted for a few minutes, fretting because Liz didn't seem to need him at all. He finally went into the waiting room and sat down in the recliner. The TV was on with the volume turned down low. He flipped channels until he found the cartoon network. A Tom and Jerry cartoon was just beginning so he settled down to watch. *Pup on a Picnic*, he hadn't seen that one in years. He watched as Spike and Tyke took their picnic into the woods, with Jerry hiding in the picnic basket. He chuckled as Tom kept getting clobbered while trying to get to Jerry, and he was snoring softly by the time the ants marched away with the bananas, cookies, and Jerry, hiding inside a peanut butter sandwich.

Eleanor sat in the recliner beside her daughter's bed and held her hand until Liz slept too. Two hours later, a nurse came in to unhook the almost empty IV drip. Even the beeping sound didn't wake either of them. She smiled as she saw their locked hands and remembered the times in her life when she had needed her own mother. The bond between a mother and daughter can fix most anything.

CHAPTER 30

"**A**s one whom his mother comforts, I will comfort you; and you shall be comforted in Jerusalem"

- Isaiah 66:13 AKJV

The first rays of sunlight streaming into the waiting room window awakened Rock from a restful sleep. An old Scooby-Doo episode was playing on the silent screen. Someone must have come in to turn the volume down while he was sleeping. He stretched and rubbed his hand across his stubble of a beard. He needed to shave and shower in the worst way. He walked across the hall to Liz's room and peeked in. Liz was still asleep, but Eleanor was at the sink washing her face.

"She rested well the whole night," she told him. "The nurse said she would probably be released at about noon."

"Thank you for staying the night, Eleanor. She needed you much more than I realized."

Eleanor smiled. "We girls need our Mamas when we're in distress. I still miss mine."

Just then, Liz woke up and looked from one to the other of them. Rock walked across the room and kissed her lightly on the cheek. "How do you feel this morning?"

She wiggled and stretched, then put her hand on her hip. "A good bit sore this morning, but other than that I feel fine."

"Wonderful," he said. "While you're in such good hands, I'm going to run to the beach house to shower and shave. You don't want me to linger around too long. Without a shave I look like a half crazed madman."

"Yeah," she said. "I almost didn't recognize you." She wrinkled up her nose.

He laughed. "I see her spunkiness is back," he told Eleanor. "Take good care of her until I get back."

His mom, dad and both sisters were waiting for him in the kitchen when he got through showering. His mom had made a pot of coffee and fried some bacon and scrambled some eggs. "You need something to eat," she said. "I'll bet you didn't eat any dinner last night."

She was right - he had forgotten to eat and he was starved.

After breakfast, he took Zach and Jake down the beach to see what was happening. The Island News had gotten a hold of the story and a geologist was already there studying the nature of the 'footprints' on the path.

"So you and your wife are the ones who've been in the news this morning?" Jeff Westcott had introduced himself. "When I heard about the path, I had to come down and see it for myself. I had heard about it before but didn't really think it existed."

Zach was quick with his questions. "What do you think it is, and who made it?" he asked.

Jeff looked at the boy, then back at Rock. "It's my theory that Native Americans made the path using a giant shell for a mold. It's the shape of a Noble Pen Shell, which is odd, because this shell is only found in the

Mediterranean Sea. It could have been brought here from across the sea by early traders though - something to trade to the Indians in exchange for rich minerals such as gold or silver. They would have been fascinated by a shell this large and odd shaped.

"The mold would have been filled with a crushed base layer, probably ground oyster shell, sand, rock and maybe even non-porous clay - then mixed with a binding agent, I have no idea what until I analyze it." He put his tools down and looked at Rock. "It's going to be an interesting study that will take up a good part of my summer." He looked from Rock to the boys. "You don't know of any college kids that need a summer job, do you? The ones I've had for the past two years have graduated and moved on."

Zach started dancing around. "Uncle Rock! Do you think Dad...."

Rock laughed. "This one will be going to Savannah State University this Fall to study Marine Biology. From his reaction, I think he might be interested."

"Well I'm glad I asked."

"When can I start?" Zach asked excitedly. "And Jake here..."

Rock interrupted. "Hold your horses, Zach. You'll need to talk to your mom and dad."

"Oh, they won't care - I know they won't! Do you think Miss Edie would let us stay in the beach house?"

Rock laughed. "Look what you've started," Rock said to the geologist. "We've got to go back to the house now. I need to pick my wife up from the hospital." He pointed to the boys. "But I'm sure these two will be back to see you and bring my brother with them. Don't go away."

"I'll be right here when you get back," he said.

***

The suitcases were on the bed with stacks of clothes ready to be packed. Rock, Lisa and Allison had already swept, mopped and tidied up the beach house.

"Why do suitcases always seem smaller when you're packing to go home?" Liz asked as she tried to stuff the remainder of her clothes in the bag.

"Maybe it's because we're in a hurry to be there," Rock said. He was having the same trouble with his.

"True," she said. "I'm not packing nearly as neatly as I did when we came down. I am so ready to be back in Park Place."

Rock played over in his mind the events of the last few days. It had been a horrific ordeal for Liz. His own stress and worry over her condition had taken a toll on him as well. It had been an idyllic, peaceful vacation for both of them up until Liz's kidnapping.

He stopped his packing and reached for her. He gathered her into his arms and enjoyed the feeling of her rounded belly between them, the sweet little life that had sprouted from the seed of their love for one another.

She smiled up at him. "There's a large basketball between us, keeping me from melting in your arms," she said teasingly.

"Just think, though. That basketball will be bouncing around in both our arms soon." She leaned forward and her head settled comfortably on his shoulder. He breathed in the scent of her, wondering why her hair always smelled like a tree full of apple blossoms. He couldn't get enough of it.

He was amazed that she could still tease and be playful after her ordeal. He held her back and looked in her eyes. "Liz, I'm sorry our vacation had to end the way it did. It was wonderful while it lasted. You added a whole new dimension to vacationing with my family - I've never been so happy."

"It was out of our control, Rock. And I refuse to let the last two days define what our time together meant to me. Your family is wonderful - such warm and generous spirits. I'm glad I got to know them better."

"I felt the same about your mom. I knew you were close, but I didn't understand the close bond you shared until I saw her in action. She's a wonderful caregiver."

"She's had enough practice. She's the oldest of her doorstep siblings - every two years her mom had her babies, finally stopping with Uncle Pete. She was the main caregiver of my grandmother, then my grandfather in their final days."

She pulled away from him. "You need to leave me alone, Reverend Clark," she said. "We'll never get on the road if you keep pulling me in your arms."

He held up his arms. "I promise, nothing but gentle hugs for the next couple of weeks." He gave her a quick kiss on the lips. "And a lingering kiss here and there. I love you Elizabeth Clark!"

"And don't I know it," she said. "If anything, our ordeal has pulled us closer together. The way you suffered too made me realize just how much you love me." She gave him a quick kiss back.

"Knock, knock."

"It's Charlie," he said. "Let me go see what he wants. I'll be right back and carry the suitcases down to the car."

Charlie was standing at the kitchen door with some sort of contraption in his hands when Rock opened the door. Liz had followed Rock to the door.

"Hey Charlie," she said. "Are you going to miss all the excitement we brought with us?" she teased.

"Hey Cupcake," he said, leaning over to hug her. "I'm glad you're alright. Macie and I have been worried sick." He sniffed her hair. "You smell like apple blossoms." he said.

She and Rock both laughed. "I've heard that one before," she said. "Thank you."

"What's that you've got?" Rock asked, looking at the rope and pulley contraption Charlie had dropped on the deck floor when he hugged Liz.

Charlie looked proudly at the thing on the deck. "It's a pulley system I invented to raise and lower things from our porch to the ground below. These beach houses built on stilts are not easy on an old man's knees. You can use it to lower your suitcases. I noticed when y'all checked in that you had a ton of stuff to haul up the steps. It'll be easier to lower them down with this."

Liz tried not to laugh, but couldn't help herself. Rock rolled his eyes at her. "I think he's referring to you as an old man," she said.

Charlie looked embarrassed. "No, no," he said. "Just figured I would make myself useful."

"And you are," Rock said, picking up the pulley and looking it over. "I was dreading those steps," he said trying to ease the older man's mind. He didn't want to disappoint him by telling him he had already enlisted the help of the teenagers in the family. They had promised to come when he started carrying things down, but they would enjoy seeing the contraption operate. "How does this thing work?"

Charlie started hooking it up on the deck rails, looking rather pleased with himself. "It's been a lifesaver for me and Macie," he said, and started demonstrating it as soon as Rock brought him one of Liz's shopping bags.

"You should patent this," Rock said. Charlie beamed with pride, and so did Liz as she watched how kind her husband was, accepting Charlie's help when he didn't really need it. She offered up a silent 'thank you' to God one more time for bringing this good man into her life.

CHAPTER 31

"*Casting all your anxieties on him, because he cares for you.*"

- 1 Peter 5:7 ESV

"Thank God you're back!" Rock had called Reva to tell her they were coming home a day earlier than expected and she was waiting for them, sitting on a bench in the courtyard when Rock drove into the garage. She jumped up and ran to greet Liz when Rock opened her door. "Here, Miss Liz, let me help you walk inside." She reached for her hand.

"Reva, she's fine. She doesn't need any help."

She turned her gaze on Rock, and put her hands on her hips. "Really?" She gave him a staredown. "And how would you know, you skinny little man? You don't have a stomach the size of a watermelon that you have to lug around. And after such a long ride, it's hard to get up."

Liz snickered and when Reva held her hand out again, she took it and let Reva help her out of the SUV. "Thank you, Reva." She turned to Rock and threw her head back. "Yes, really?" she said as if she were snubbing him. "How would you know, you skinny little man?" He looked at her in astonishment. She winked at him.

"Lord help me," Rock said, as he closed the door behind them and ran to open the door to the house. "They're ganging up on me."

Reva got Liz settled in the recliner as Rock kept going back for bags and suitcases. "It smells so good in here," Liz said.

"Holly came over and dusted this morning. She sprayed some air freshener - said it might be a little musty after being closed up for almost two weeks. She said she would be over when you get settled and bring Theo home."

"Did Theo give them any trouble?" Rock asked.

"She didn't say, but I expect he did, the little rascal," Reva said.

"I'm afraid to ask her," he said.

"He was a perfect angel," Holly said when she came over. "The first few days, he wandered around meowing and looking for you, but after that, he resigned himself to the fact that we were all he had, and he'd better be nice." She laughed. "Well, there was a little mishap or two. He kept jumping on the back of Dan's office chair and knocking things off the bookshelf behind him, but we finally just took everything off the shelf and he was fine."

Theo was giving Rock his evil eye. "Come on, old boy. Jump on my lap. We missed you." Theo ignored him. "I know how to get his attention," he said. He walked in the kitchen and snapped the top off of a can of catfood. Theo came running over, weaving his body in and out of Rock's legs.

"Totally controlled by his stomach," Rock said and poured some into his bowl.

"I know the feeling," Liz said and sighed. "I think I need a nap."

"You might want to wait - Mom's bringing dinner over in a few minutes."

Rock and Liz exchanged glances. They were both thinking the same thing - how quickly Holly had transitioned from calling her mother-in-law by her name to now calling her Mom. He knew Maura must be thrilled. She loved her daughter-in-law dearly.

"Where's Abby?" Liz asked.

"She's helping Mom," she said. "They're two peas in a pod."

Rock laughed. "Two peas in a pod. Holly, if I didn't know better, I'd think you were a southern gal."

"It's growing on me," she said. She glanced out the window. "Here they come now. Notice it when they come in - Abby even has an apron like Mom's. She's teaching her how to sew." She turned back from the window. Rock noticed that her eyes were full of tears. She sat down on the ottoman in front of Liz. "I can't believe I waited so long to find my family," she said.

Liz reached out and held her hand. "It's all in God's timing," she said. "Look at me and Rock. He timed things perfectly for us."

When Rock had called Reva earlier in the day to let her know they were coming home, he asked her if she would spread the word to everyone not to talk about the events of the last few days. He was glad now that he had. Liz was back in her own little world with the people she loved, and she seemed to be putting the stress behind her. Holly and Rock had cleaned up the table and washed the dishes as she and Maura had chatted about the neighborhood, Abby's puppy who was growing into a huge dog, and about the things Abby and her friends had been doing since school let out.

By the time he had washed his face and brushed his teeth, Liz had sacked out and was sound asleep when he got into bed. He cuddled up to her and put his arm around her. It was the most wonderful feeling and he wondered how many more days it would be just the two of them. How would this little boy that God had blessed them with change their relationship. He smiled as he felt a stirring under his hand. "We'll be just fine," he said.

Liz turned over on her back. "Um, can't get comfortable," she said.

"Can I help in any way?" he asked. "Another pillow, maybe?" When she didn't answer, he realized she was talking in her sleep.

CHAPTER 32

"*Rejoice with them that do rejoice, and weep with them that weep.*"

- Romans 12:15

It felt good to walk into church, sit on the back pew and listen while someone else gave the sermon. He and Liz were greeted warmly by everyone, but no one mentioned their vacation. Rock was touched by Ned's sermon and on the way out, he complimented him. "And I've heard a lot of good things," Rock told him. "Reva seems ready to boot me out and take you in."

Ned laughed. "I think she just likes to feed me. Fatten me up, she says."

"So that's it! She was like that with me until I got married. I just knew I would lose a few pounds when she stopped cooking for me, but Liz took up where she left off. She's a good cook too. But seriously, Ned, everyone has been singing your praises. You've done a fine job."

"I know they've missed you, but they've been very gracious to me. You've got a wonderful church here - and good people. If you're ever able to hire an associate, I would be very interested."

"We'll talk," Rock said. "Come by my office tomorrow."

"Thank you, Rock. I'll call Reva and make an appointment."

"Green beans, tomatoes and cucumbers all straight from the garden." Cap Price put the basket down on the kitchen counter. Madge walked in behind him. "And don't forget the squash. We've made you a squash casserole and some green beans already cooked. Betty Ann's bringing a chicken pot pie. Rev Rock, you can slice the tomatoes and cucumbers and lunch will be ready."

"Y'all are spoiling me," Liz said. "I'm fine though, I really am."

Madge put her arm around her and leaned in for a hug. "From what you've been through child, you deserve to be spoiled." She looked from Liz to Rock. "I know we're not supposed to talk about it, but if we ignore what happened, Liz will think we don't care."

"So that's why no one has mentioned it," Liz said. "I was beginning to feel a little uncomfortable as if there was something being left unsaid. I could see the empathy in everyone's eyes but no one spoke of it." She turned to Rock. "I know you're just trying to protect me, Rock. You're right that I don't want to delve into the details, but it's okay to at least acknowledge that it happened." She turned back to Madge. "It was stressful, Madge, and thank you for caring!"

Betty Ann walked in with the chicken pot pie. "It's hot," she said. "I had the timer set while we were at church and it dinged right when I walked back in the door."

Rock went to the cabinet door. "I'll set the table," he said. "I hope you'll all stay and help us eat!"

"We can't stay," Madge said. "Cap promised me he would take me to the new Asian restaurant in Sparta."

"Neither can I," Betty said. She sat the pot pie down on the stovetop. "You'll have plenty for leftovers."

***

There was a stack of addressed and stamped envelopes on the edge of Reva's desk when Rock walked in the office on Monday morning. It was church bulletins, ready to be mailed to the shut-ins.

"Business as usual, I see," he said.

She smiled. "Some things never change. By the way, Ned will be here at 10:30. He said you told him to come by and I imagine he wants to update you on what's happened since you've been away."

"Good! I feel like I've been gone a month instead of eleven days. Reva, I want you to get a hold of as many elders as possible while I sort through the things on my desk. I've written everything on this note. Read it to them and ask them for a yes or no."

She looked at the note. "Hallelujah! I'll get on it right away. I'll email everyone first. If they don't respond, I'll call them. Oh, and would you mind taking these bulletins to the post office this morning? I need to get them off my desk so I can get some work done."

"I guess so. I dread going in there now that Betty's gone. Have they hired someone yet? There'll never be another Betty."

"I suppose so," she said. "Ned's been going to the post office and hasn't said. He's been picking up your personal mail too. It's all on your desk."

"Well, I guess I'll find out. I might as well get it over with." He was despondent as he picked up the bulletins and headed out the door. Reva watched him leave with his shoulders drooping.

Several people he knew were walking out the door of the post office, talking and laughing. He felt indignant. How could they laugh when the heart of Park Place was being ripped out from under them. Betty, the self-appointed Mayor, dog catcher, and neighborhood crime watch chairman was being snatched away into retirement after thirty years on the job. Park Place would never be the same.

He used his key to open up the church's box and then opened up his own. A large envelope stood out - a high school graduation announcement from Zach. They had given him his present at the beach. He stood at the small table and sorted through his other mail - bills, junk mail, a flyer from Junie's Feed and Seed store. He skimmed the addresses - Reverend Rockford Clark, Mrs. Liz Clark, Mr. and Mrs. Rockford W. Clark. What a difference a year makes, he thought. Mr. and Mrs., Reverend and Mrs. - he would never get tired of seeing it. Last year at this time, he was sitting on the porch of the cottage drinking iced tea with his friend. This year she was his wife and about to have his child. "Thank you, Lord," he said out loud.

"Who's that prayin' in my lobby," came a loud and familiar voice from inside the post office. "It sounds like the beach bum preacher. Get yourself in here."

It was Betty - what was she doing here? he wondered. Oh yeah - probably training someone. He walked in and looked around, but only saw Betty and Wanda Burns.

Betty wasn't behind the counter. She and Wanda were in front of the counter and Wanda was hugging her. He was relieved. He didn't feel like meeting the new postal clerk today.

"What's wrong - is the work so hard, the new person quit on you already?" he asked. "How did your retirement party go?"

Betty smiled at Wanda. "Oh, it was wonderful - there was over a hundred people there. They roasted me."

"I would have liked to have been a part of that," he said. "I could have come up with some good stuff." He looked around again. "But what about the new clerk that's taking your place. Where is she?"

Betty looked at him with a very serious and sad expression. "We had to let her go." She sighed. "You just can't find good help anymore."

"Seriously?" Rock asked. " You were impressed with her when you interviewed her, weren't you? Now what are we going to do?"

Wanda started to say something, but Betty interrupted. "Miss Wanda, you just keep your mouth shut."

"Yes, Ma'am," Wanda replied, and made a zipping motion on her lips.

Rock looked from one to the other and Betty batted her eyes at him.

"Tsk - you're just going to have to put up with me, that's what."

Now he was confused. "What does that mean?"

"They're letting me come back!" Betty grabbed his hand and Wanda's and started jumping up and down with Wanda joining in. He couldn't help but be caught up in the action and before he knew it, he was jumping up and down with them. The door opened and in walked Walt Helms, the pastor of Cornerstone Baptist Church. Rock stopped abruptly. He realized how foolish he must look and besides, he didn't even know what he was dancing about.

"Don't stop on my account," Walt said. "If you're auditioning for something, you need a little more practice - especially Rev Rock, here." He grabbed Rock's hand. "Here, let me show you how it's done. I took ballroom dancing lessons in high school."

Rock jerked his hand loose. "I've had enough dancing lessons for the day, thank you. And I prefer to dance with the ladies if I have to dance."

Betty and Wanda were bent over double laughing.

Walt and Rock laughed at their laughing. "This is a zoo," Rock finally said. "You'd never know we were in an official government office."

"Oops," said Betty, and ran behind the counter. "Somebody might come in."

"Somebody's already in," Walt said. "Don't we count?"

"Wait a minute," Rock said. "Would someone please tell me what we were dancing about. I just got back into town, and the post office has turned into a dance hall. Am I left out of the loop, or what?"

The door opened from the back where the the mail carrier delivered the daily mail. "Just a minute Brian. I'm trying to explain something to my customers. I'll be right there."

She faced the counter again. "I just told you Rev Rock - I'm not leaving. They're letting me stay!"

"But you retired." Was she pulling his leg? She just said she had a retirement party.

"That's what I'm trying to tell you. I retired but now I've unretired. I just found out this morning."

"I don't think unretired is a word," said Wanda.

"And I want to know what that means," said Rock.

Walt raised his hand. "Me too."

"Shush up, all of you. Just let me explain."

"Please do," Walt and Rock said in unison.

"Y'all know how sick I was over retiring. I thought I had made a huge mistake." They all nodded. "And especially when I found out they were going to cut back and change the post office hours to just four hours a day?" They nodded again. "Well, I asked them if I could come back since now the hours would be part time. At first they said no, the paperwork was already done and it was out of the question." They all nodded once again.

"Y'all don't have to keep noddin'." They nodded anyway. "Dad-burnit. I don't even know why I asked to come back. You are all crazy." She shook her head. "But anyway, I just found out this morning that they've cancelled my retirement and lettin' me stay! I had just finished telling Wanda. That's why we were dancing!"

"I feel like dancing again," Rock said. "But I'll refrain this time."

"Thank goodness," Walt said.

"Wait just a minute!" A big voice boomed from behind Betty. Everyone got still and looked in the direction of the voice.

"Oh, Brian, did you hear my announcement?"

"I did. But you had a retirement party and everybody gave you great stuff. Come to think of it, I think you just faked your retirement so you could get gifts and have people say nice things about you - kinda like being able to go to your own funeral."

"I did no such thing! I did retire and I just found out today that I'm unretired."

"Uh, that's not a word," Wanda said again.

"Shush," said Betty.

Brian started talking loudly again. "You know you have to give it all back, don't you? All the gift cards, presents... well everything. It's proper etiquette."

Betty's mouth dropped open. "But I've already used most of the gift cards." She sounded genuinely worried. "I can't give back what I've already used."

"Cough up the money, honey. I'm expectin' mine back. Hmm...I think I gave you $10 in an envelope."

"You did not! You just came to the party to eat, you old con man. You didn't give me a dime."

"Dang it! I thought I was going to get ten bucks off you." He laughed. "Darlin', you don't have to give nothin' back. Everybody's so happy that you're going to get to stay, they would probably throw you a welcome home party."

"The only way y'all gonna get rid of me is if I die." she said.

"Huh-uh." Brian took her by the arm and led her to the window. "You see that shovel on the back stoop?" She nodded. "When you die, they're just going to dig a hole and put you in it. Then they can say you loved the Park Place Post Office so much you never left."

"And then I'll come back and haunt you," she said.

"Well, I'm just glad I didn't go to the retirement party - probably saved me fifty bucks," Rock said. Betty's indignant expression got the best of him and he laughed. "No, really Betty, I'm sure everyone is just as happy as I am that you're not going anywhere for a while. We'll have to send a thank you card to the post office personnel department."

"Amen," said Walt. He looked at Rock. "By the way, I heard what happened to Liz. Our church has had a prayer chain going."

"Ours too," Betty piped in. "I hope she's going to be okay."

"What happened?" Wanda asked. "I haven't heard."

"Well, you're the only one in town that hasn't," Betty said. "You keep your head in the sand writing that second book of yours and you don't keep up with the news."

Walt saw the expression on Rock's face and knew he wasn't up to repeating the ordeal again. "You just go on, Rock. I know you've got stuff to do after being gone. I'll fill Wanda in - it'll be one more prayer being lifted up."

"Thank you Walt. We can always use one more prayer."

***

Rock started to go straight back to work, but remembered that it had been at least a month since he had sent Liz flowers. After all she'd been through, he wanted to do something special. He passed by the Feed and Seed Store and peeked in. It was 10:15 and he had forgotten all about his Monday morning meeting with the boys. He didn't have time to stop in since he was meeting with Ned at 10:30. He hoped he could get by unnoticed and he did.

The bell rang as he stepped into May's Flower Shop, and he heard her familiar voice. "Come on back, Rev Rock. I'm working on a wreath for Martha Staton's front door." He walked to the back where May was working. "It always smells so good in here," he commented.

"It's a mixture of the fresh flowers, the scented candles and the homemade sugar cookies I put out this morning for my favorite customers."

"I hope I made the list," he said reaching for one.

"At the very top," she said. "What can I help you with today?"

"How about something with a huge wow factor for Liz?"

"I heard about what happened and I'm so sorry. Is she okay?"

"She's fine physically but she's still a little stressed. She doesn't say so, but I can tell."

"Who wouldn't be?" she said. "I think I have just the thing for her. I got some fabulous hydrangeas in today. The blossoms are the biggest and the bluest I've ever seen. Blue is supposed to be a calming color."

"Perfect," he said. "You always seem to know exactly what she likes."

"Oh, and I got some cute new baby stuff too - some of those soft cuddly books and stuffed animals. "How about if I wrap something up for the baby for a nice touch. They're in the box by the back door. Go pick something out. It's on the house."

Rock walked over and came back with plastic bag holding a soft cloth book and a stuffed monkey.

"Curious George. Perfect," she said. "When do you want it delivered?"

"Can you wait until I get there. I should be home and through with dinner by 6."

"That's about the time I leave the shop. I'll bring it by on my way home."

Ned was waiting for him when he returned to the office. He had packed up the few items he had brought with him and had them in a bag ready to carry out to the car.

"Ned, I need to see Reva in my office before we get started. When she comes out, you can come on in. It won't take us but a few minutes."

Ned laughed. "Take all the time you need," he said. "I don't have anywhere I need to be. I'm out of a job, remember?"

Reva closed the door behind her. "Jim Reed was the only one I couldn't get a hold of. Everyone else said yes."

"Thanks Reva. Just email Jim and tell him we have a quorum and the deed's done, and now send Ned in."

"With pleasure."

Ned sat down and pulled out his notebook. "Here's the list of who I visited in the hospital and some of the calls I got. I have a more detailed report that I'm planning to email to you." He handed the notebook to Rock.

"And I've got something for you to look over." He pulled out the job description for the Youth Pastor position. The Session had approved it a month ago after a generous donation had been received for that express purpose, and they had just now approved Ned for the job.

"What's this?" Ned asked.

"We're offering it to you if you agree with the salary and the terms," Rock said. "I think you'll be perfect for the job."

"Hallelujah!" Ned said. "My prayers have been answered."

"I think you've been around Reva too long," Rock said, and got up from his seat to shake Ned's hand.

CHAPTER 33

"*Have I not commanded you? Be strong and courageous. Do not be frightened, and do not be dismayed, for the Lord your God is with you wherever you go.*"

- Joshua 1:9

"Dr. Anderson's office called today."

"We have an appointment with him on Friday, don't we?

"They've moved it to tomorrow instead. Your Uncle Joe called Dr. Anderson and filled him in on my hospital visit, so he wants me to come in early."

"That's good. I'm glad he's so thorough."

Rock got a second helping from the casserole dish on the table. "I think Betty Ann's chicken pot pie is better the second time around." He looked at Liz's plate. "You haven't eaten much. Can I get you something different?"

"No, I'm just not very hungry."

He poured himself another glass of tea.

"Rock?"

"Yes?" He looked up at her expectantly and could tell right away something was wrong. "What is it, Liz. Are you not feeling well?" He got up from the table and went and knelt by her chair. "What's wrong?"

"I'm scared."

"Why, what are you afraid of?" He was going into panic mode and he knew it. He had to make himself calm down.

"The baby," she let out a sniffle, and used her napkin to wipe her eyes. "He's still not moving as much as he was before all this happened. I'm afraid something's wrong with him."

"Wait," he said. "I was reading something this morning in the baby book. Let me go get it." He ran in the study and got the book. He pulled his chair around the table to sit beside Liz.

"Here, this is it." He started reading. "At around 38 weeks, *you may notice a reduction in the number of movements you feel - your baby is likely to have quite distinct periods of inactivity and longer periods of sleep. As the baby gets bigger, the movements feel different because they have less space to move in.*"

She reached over and hugged him. "I love you. Maybe that's it," she said. "I've just been so worried that all that banging around has hurt him somehow, even though the ultrasound showed that it didn't." She kissed him on the lips. "I know I'm a worrywort. It's just one of those feelings that won't let go."

"It's a good thing they moved your appointment up. I'm sure Dr. Anderson will ease your mind."

As soon as Rock started clearing off the table, the doorbell rang.

"Who could that be?" Liz asked.

"I don't know. I'll go to the door."

"No, I'll get it. You have soap suds on your hands."

He heard her exclaim as she opened the door, "Oh my, those are the most beautiful flowers I've ever seen, May. I love hydrangeas – and they're a periwinkle blue – my favorite color. Who are they from?"

"Open the card and see," May told her. "And there's a small package to go with it." Liz reached for the basket. "I'll carry it, Liz. It's heavy - it's a potted plant. You can plant it in your flower garden when the blooms start fading."

"Well, come on in the kitchen, then. You can put it on the table - Rock's clearing away the supper dishes."

Rock dried his hands on a dish towel while Liz opened the card. She read it and looked up at him. "You rascal - I should have known it was from you." She winked at him. "And it couldn't have come at a better time." She put the card on the table. "There's a package too! I love surprises!"

She unwrapped the box and opened it. "Oh, Curious George - You know how I love George." She gave Rock an affectionate smile. "And a Curious George book to go along with it." She glanced up at May. "I started reading to the baby a couple of months ago - it was when he was so active and kicking so much. It seemed to calm him down. These cloth books are great - he can even keep it in the crib."

"I just got the shipment this morning and Rock came into the shop right after it arrived." She glanced at him and nodded. "I think he made a good choice."

"So do I. Don't I have the most thoughtful husband in the world?"

May laughed. "I don't know about the world, but you've sure got the most thoughtful one in Park Place. We need about twenty just like him and May's Flower Shop would be booming."

Rock noticed that Liz had both hands holding the underside of her stomach. "Liz, do you feel okay? You're not having contractions, are you? I see you're holding your stomach."

"No, it just feels heavy - like I need to hold it up." She laughed. "But of course, it is heavy. I think I've got a future linebacker in here. I wonder what he weighs now?"

"How about we get you settled in the recliner with your feet up. That'll take some of the pressure off."

"Good idea. May, you should sit down with us for a while."

"No, I need to get home, but thank you for asking. You and the little linebacker will be in my prayers." Rock walked her to the door. "Thanks again for the business, Rock."

"Don't worry, I'll be calling you again soon," he said, as she walked out the door.

"It's chilly in here. I'm shivering."

"I'll turn the A/C up a notch." He walked to the hallway to the thermostat and when he came back, he was carrying a small blanket. He wrapped it around her and tucked the bottom under her feet. He turned the small lamp on and brought her the book she had been reading. "Is that better?"

"Much better, thank you - you're so good to me."

She turned to the bookmarked page and started reading. He sat on the sofa and opened up the newspaper. He skimmed the front page and then turned to the *Around Town* page that listed birth announcements and weddings.

"Hey Liz," he said. "Did you know that your old principal, Beth Perkins, is getting married again?" When she didn't answer, he looked up and saw that she was already asleep. He got up and went into his study. May as well get a head start on Sunday's sermon - two Sundays without having to preach and he was feeling a little out of practice.

After an hour of working on his outline, he walked back into the living room to check on Liz. She had gone to bed while he'd been working on his sermon. He worked for another hour, but he couldn't concentrate. He was worried about Liz. Was she right - could there be something wrong with the baby? And she was so tired.

He opened up his laptop and googled 'pregnancy'. Hundreds of things popped up. He opened his email account. They had subscribed to a website that sent emails each week about what to expect at each stage. He had opened them eagerly each week. He had never thought there would come a time when he would be glued to the computer each week reading about baby development, and more recently labor pains and dilation.

There it was - Your Baby at 37 Weeks. Week 37 was really not much different from Week 36, except each additional week in the womb served to strengthen the baby's lungs. He chuckled when he thought about how much sound can come out of a tiny baby's lungs. There was proof of that during the occasional church service when a crying baby gave his sermon some stiff competition.

Tired and sluggish - this was what he had been looking for. *The sluggish feeling comes from carrying all the excess pounds, from your over-active bladder and from bad sleeping positions. In addition, your growing baby puts more pressure on major blood vessels making less oxygen available to your brain.*

All her symptoms seemed to be normal. He was relieved. As he read, he was reminded about how different it would be in the house with a baby and he prayed a simple prayer. "Lord, you are giving us a gift and we are thankful - the gift of a child that each of us in our own separate worlds have always longed for, but neither of us dreamed possible. You have chosen to bless our union - our joining together with this gift and I pray that we can raise this child up in a way that will be satisfactory to you. Be with Liz as her body undergoes the changes necessary for childbirth. Protect her and the baby from harm. And Lord, give me the strength and courage to face any trials there may be and help me to be a good husband and father. In your Son's name I pray. Amen."

When he finally went to bed, he tossed and turned for a while, not able to go to sleep. A thunderstorm had come and gone and he could hear the rumbling of the thunder as it continued its path to the east, wetting the thirsty crops along the way. Sleep came and with it, vivid dreams, noisy dreams. A dog barking, a baby crying and a sound of distress so near the edge of his dream world, it seemed real. What finally pulled him from his dream was not the noise, but a shaking of his shoulder, then his name being called. He jumped and sat straight up in bed.

"Rock, honey - get up. I'm in so much pain."

"What is it? Liz, what's wrong Are you in labor?"

She moaned. "I don't think so. It hurts so bad - something's wrong - I'm sure of it. Can you help me to the bathroom?

He jumped up and turned on the light. He went around to her side of the bed and helped her into a sitting position, her moaning in pain the whole while. When she stood up, he gasped. There was blood on the sheets - a lot. This wasn't supposed to happen. He had read all about the water breaking and what you should expect, but this wasn't it. This was bad. He eased her back on the bed.

"Liz, stay here - I'm calling an ambulance."

She didn't argue, and slumped back on her pillow.

CHAPTER 34

"*Fear not for I am with you; Be not dismayed, for I am your God. I will strengthen you, Yes, I will help you. I will uphold you with my righteous right hand.*"

- Isaiah 41:10

Lonnie Welch was the EMS driver on duty and Rock was glad of it. He brought the stretcher inside the house and handled Liz as carefully as he would a fragile flower. They made it to the hospital in record time and wheeled her through the large emergency room doors. They zipped her down the hallway to an examining room. Rock remembered bringing another pregnant woman through the doors in his arms just six months before when Maria Ramirez had fainted in BJ's diner. He was concerned that time, but this time he was frantic with worry. This was his Liz and something was definitely wrong. Nowhere in the baby book had they mentioned blood.

Dr. Anderson was not on call, but he gave instructions over the phone when they called him and told them to move her to the maternity floor for a 3D ultrasound. He made it into the room within fifteen minutes after he was called. He must sleep in his clothes, Rock thought as he looked him over, slightly rumpled but fully dressed. Bless him!

They had already hooked up the fetal heart rate monitor. As he was doing the ultrasound he continuously watched the monitor. Three minutes in, he yelled at the nurses. "Prep her for a c-section, stat!"

They wheeled her out as Rock watched helplessly. Liz was asleep or sedated - he didn't know which, but he knew if he didn't sit down soon, he was going to be joining her, but for him it would be on the floor. Dr. Anderson took him by the arm. "Let's go in this office, Rock. I need to tell you what's going on."

"Please do," he said.

Mitch Anderson gave him a cup of water from the cooler after he had seated him on the couch. He sat down beside him. "I can't stay but a minute. I have to get back to Liz." He took a deep breath and Rock knew it was serious - very serious by the expression on his face.

"She has something called placental abruption," he said. "It's more often than not caused by trauma to the abdomen or a fall, which I understand from talking to your brother, this happened last week. It's a serious condition where the placenta separates from the uterus before the baby is born and it's dangerous for both Liz and the baby. The baby is already in distress which is why I ordered an immediate c-section."

At Rock's crestfallen face, Dr. Anderson continued. "Son, I hated like the dickens to tell you this, but I had to give you the worst news first."

"Now I'll give you the good news. First: It's a partial separation - not a complete one. The baby is still getting some nutrients and oxygen. Second: The baby is otherwise healthy. His lungs seem to be fully developed, he's at least a six pounder and not considered premature at all. Third: It was caught early and you came to the hospital without delay, so Liz hasn't lost a huge amount of blood. I understand she had to be given a unit of blood last week?"

"Yes, she did. And her blood type isn't very common - will that be a problem if she needs more?"

"No, I've already had Mary at the nurse's station check. We have a good supply here. They should have her prepped by now. I have to get back there. Dr. Samuels will be assisting me." He turned to go.

"Doctor Anderson, was she asleep just now or was she unconscious?"

"Neither, she squeezed my hand. She was awake and aware - she just had her eyes closed. I think she was just trying to preserve her energy. I've seen a lot of pregnant women do just that when there's an emergency – it's nature's way. We'll be giving her an epidural for the surgery. We won't sedate her because of the baby being under stress already."

"Can I go back and be with her?"

"No. During a normal c-section, I sometimes say yes, but this is an emergency and you would just be in the way."

Rock felt lost. "What can I do?"

"You can do what you do best, pray."

"Only if you do what you do best - and do it the best you possibly can."

"Deal." Dr. Anderson shook his hand. Rock walked straight to the waiting room. There was one woman sitting in a chair dozing. Rock wouldn't have cared if there'd been a circus ringmaster and two lion tamers in there. He got down on his knees and prayed. He realized it sounded more like a whine than a prayer, "Lord, you promised ......

Twenty-five minutes later, he was still on his knees when Dr. Anderson walked through the door. He walked over and put his hand on Rock's shoulder. When he stood up, the sudden movement made him dizzy, and now, after feeling light headed ever since he had first seen the bloody sheets on their bed, he passed out...cold.

CHAPTER 35

"*R*ejoice in the Lord always; again I will say, Rejoice."
                                    - Philippians 4:4

The next thing Rock knew, a nurse was seated on the floor beside him. "Mr. Clark, wake up. Let's get you off the floor and lay you down on the couch here."

He looked around, feeling extremely foolish. Dr. Anderson was still in the room. He got up with the nurse's help and sat on the sofa. "I'm okay now."

Dr. Anderson sat down beside him. "I was trying to give you some good news. I didn't expect you to conk out on me." He smiled.

"Good news?"

"Yes. Liz and your seven pound, 9 ounce baby boy are both doing fine."

"Oh, thank you God!" he said, looking up at the ceiling.

"Thank him indeed," Mitch said. "We'll be monitoring Liz, but I don't think she'll need blood. She must not have lost quite as much as you thought."

"It looked like a lot," he said.

"I'm glad you got here right away. It made all the difference in the world."

"You didn't do so shabby yourself. Do you ever sleep? Or are you just always ready to jump out of bed and get to the hospital?"

"I'm not normally quite that quick," he said. "A case like this is always an exception though. The faster we can get a c-section done, the better it is for the patients."

"Thank you! I just can't thank you enough."

Dr. Anderson smiled and winked. "You'll get a bill. Now, do you want to see your wife and baby, or not?"

Rock went running down the hallway behind the tall doctor whose long legs were heading straight to room number 312. It was one of the ten rooms on the maternity floor where he'd visited many new mothers and their babies for twenty-two years as their pastor, never as the husband or the father of a perfect baby boy sleeping peacefully in his beautiful mother's arms when he walked in the room.

Liz's face brightened when he stepped inside. She was still pale, but she smiled warmly at him. "You missed the beginning of the movie," she said. "But we're just now getting to the good part, so come on in."

His relief was staggering and his heart was overflowing. He didn't know what to do with himself. He wanted to fling his arms around Liz but he knew that was out of the question. He wanted to saturate himself with the sights and smells of his newborn son, but he didn't want to deprive Liz of the peace and serenity she must be feeling while holding him.

He sat down on the chair beside her and pulled it up as close as possible to the bed. "Does he have all his fingers and toes," he asked shyly.

"I haven't counted them yet. Why don't you hold him and we'll count them together. She reached her arms out and released her hold when she knew he had him safely in his arms. He took him tenderly from her, held him up against his chest and sighed.

"It's a new kind of love, isn't it?" she said tenderly. "A new realm of a world I didn't know existed. Do you feel it?"

"Absolutely!" he said.

"I think a prayer of thanksgiving is in order," she said.

"Absolutely!," he said again. "You start the prayer while I fill up my lungs with his sweet baby fresh smell."

Liz began the prayer and Rock ended it, both of them emotional with the tender feelings they felt for each other and their baby boy, Matthew Eli Rockford Clark.

The End

AUTHOR'S BIO

Glenda Manus lives in Van Wyck, South Carolina with her husband, Henry, and their cat, Theo. It's a small Southern community much like the fictional town of Park Place in this, her second novel. "It's a little slice of Heaven", she says. "Everyone should have the opportunity to experience small-town Southern life – if not through a real visit, then a virtual visit through the eyes and words of an author who's lived there."

Made in the USA
Columbia, SC
22 March 2018